I0527300

James McCormick Dalzell

John Gray of Mount Vernon

Vol. 1

James McCormick Dalzell

John Gray of Mount Vernon
Vol. 1

ISBN/EAN: 9783337307486

Printed in Europe, USA, Canada, Australia, Japan

Cover: Foto ©Raphael Reischuk / pixelio.de

More available books at **www.hansebooks.com**

Mount Vernon;

the

Last Soldier of the Revolution.

Born near Mount Vernon, Va., January 6, 1764;

Died at Hiramsburg, Ohio, March 29, 1868.

Aged 104 Years.

———————

"Chap. LXVIII.—An act for the Relief of John Gray, a Revolutionary Soldier.

"*Be it enacted by the Senate and House of Representatives of the United States of America, in* "*Congress assembled,* That the Secretary of the Interior be, and he is hereby, directed to place "the name of John Gray, of Noble County, Ohio, upon the Pension Roll, and that there be "paid to said John Gray, out of any money in the Treasury, not otherwise appropriated, the sum "of $500 per annum during his natural life, payable semi-annually, commencing on the 1st day "of July, 1866."

[See Statutes at Large, XXXIX Congress, Sess. II, Chap. 58, p. 44.]

HISTORY OF JOHN GRAY,

OF MOUNT VERNON, VA.,

THE LAST SOLDIER OF THE REVOLUTION.

STATE OF OHIO, EXECUTIVE DEPARTMENT,
COLUMBUS, *February* 2, 1867.

DEAR SIR: Yours of 29th ultimo is received, and the letter to the State Journal has been delivered. My duties are inconsistent with my acting as the trustee of a fund for the benefit of any private citizen, and I must beg you to find some business man or firm of known character, in the vicinity of the residence of the veteran John Gray, of the Revolution, to do that work. It would involve a good deal of correspondence which could only be intelligently done by those who are near enough to be personally cognizant of the wants and necessities of the old patriot.

Earnestly sympathizing with the spirit which induces your action,

I am, very respectfully, yours, &c.,

J. D. COX,
Governor of Ohio.

J. M. DALZELL, Esq.

[We here acknowledge ourselves much indebted to Honorable Judges Welker and Spalding, and Capt. Baugh, of Ohio, the Librarians of Congress, Heads of Departments, and many other high officials at Washington, who have aided us in the laborious task of compiling from the records of Congress and the Departments the authentic statements of this book.]

For more than three-quarters of a century after the close of the war of the Revolution, John Gray lived a life of quiet and retiracy upon or near the banks of the beautiful Ohio. He left his native Virginia, the banks of the Potomac, the home of his childhood, the State for which he had done battle service in no less a cause than the independence of that State. He left her because she denied and refused the right of suffrage to those of her sons who had not "caught Dame Fortune's golden smile," and made his home where—

> "An honest man, tho' e'er so poor,
> Is king of men for a' that."

He wended his way over mountains and rivers, through the then almost unexplored wilderness of what is now West Virginia, and coming out on the borders of Western civilization, at Morgantown, Va., he constructed a rude craft, on which he descended the Monongahela to its junction with the Alleghany, and thence down the Ohio to the Flats of Grave Creek. Here he made his first settlement, and entered with ardor upon the duties of frontier life, having for his companions in toil, privation, hardship, and frontier warfare, such men as the Poes, Wetzel, Hughs, Wheeler, Boone, Kenton, and others, who have made their names conspicuous in the annals of the West. Time rolled on, and the beautiful region "north-west of the River Ohio" was, in the year 1802, erected into a State, and John Gray, after changing his residence once or twice, settled down on the waters of Duck Creek, a tributary of the Muskingum, within the present limits of Noble (then Washington) county, in the new, free, and prosperous State of Ohio.

Here, for nearly threescore years and ten, he lived and studied. He lived to see the almost unbroken wilderness "blossom as the rose," and Ohio proudly take her position, the third State in the American Union. He lived to see men born upon the soil grow up and take the highest positions, military, civil, and ecclesiastic, in the land, men of whom any State or nation might well be proud. He lived to witness the most wonderful achievements of science of any age or any nation in his own country. He saw the majestic steamboat take the place of the frail canoe upon her lakes and rivers. He saw the giant locomotive drag the ponderous train over the highest peaks of the Alleghanies, through tunnels under mountains, over rivers and plains, through forests and prairies, and to the very summit of the Rocky Mountains. He lived to see the inventions of Franklin and Morse distance time in the transmission of intelligence from London to New York, and crossing the continent to San Francisco, return the answer to New York just as old Father Time reached the shores of America.

During all this time John Gray had neither sought nor obtained from the Government any recognition of his services in the war of the Revolution. Never rich, indeed poor in purse, he was yet too proud to ask a richly-merited annuity, and it was not till the frosts of a hundred winters had whitened his locks, and age, decrepitude, and want invaded his citadel, that he gave a reluctant consent for his friends to apply for a pension.

On the first day of the second session of the Thirty-ninth Congress, December 3, 1866, Hon. John A. Bingham, a member of the House of Representatives from the 16th district, than whom Ohio has not a brighter star in her galaxy of living statesmen, arose in his place and introduced House bill No. 835, for the relief of John Gray, a soldier of the Revolution, which was read a first and second time, and referred to the Committee on Invalid Pensions. (See page 6, Congressional Globe, second session, 39th Congress.)

On Thursday, December 13, 1866, ten days after the introduction of the bill, Mr. McIndoe, from the Committee on Revolutionary Pensions, reported back, with a recommendation that it do not pass, House bill No. 835, for the relief of John Gray, and the bill was laid on the table. (See Congressional Globe, 2d session, 39th Congress, page 3.)

Nothing daunted, the patriotic and indefatigable Bingham, after introducing the most incontestable proofs of identity of which the case would admit after the lapse of so many years, in which the old patriot had "outlived the generation born with him," on Friday, January 25, 1867, succeeded in getting a bill reported (No. 1044) by Mr. Price, from the Committee on Revolutionary Pensions, "for the relief of John Gray, which was read a first and second time. It directed the Secretary of the Interior to place the name of John Gray on the pension roll at the rate of $200 per annum, payable semi-annually." "Mr. Delano, of Ohio, inquired whether the bill had the approbation of any Committee." He was answered by Mr. Price "that it had the approbation of the Committee on Revolutionary Pensions." "This applicant," said Mr. Price, "is one hundred and three years old, and I have another similar case to report, in which the applicant is one hundred and seven years old, (referring to the case of F. D. Bakeman, of New York, since deceased,) and both these men are supported by public charity."

Mr. Spalding, of Ohio, moved to amend the bill by striking out "two hundred dollars" and inserting in lieu thereof five hundred dollars, and the amendment was agreed to. The bill was then ordered to be engrossed, and it was accordingly read a third time and passed.

" Mr. Bingham then moved to reconsider the vote by which the bill passed, and also moved to lay the motion to reconsider on the table. The latter motion was agreed to." (See Congressional Globe, 2d session, 39th Congress, page 754.)

On the same day, January 25, 1867, a message was received in the Senate from the House of Representatives by its Chief Clerk, Mr. Lloyd, announcing among other things that the House had passed bill No. 1044, for the relief of John Gray, a Revolutionary soldier, which, with others, was twice read by its title and referred to the Committee on Pensions. (See Congressional Globe, 2d session, 39th Congress, page 730.)

On Wednesday, January 30, 1867, in the Senate, Mr. Lane, from the Committee on Pensions, reported without amendment House bill No. 1044, for the relief of John Gray, a soldier of the Revolution. (See Congressional Globe, 2d session, 39th Congress, page 853.)

On February 14, 1867, " in the Senate, on motion of Mr. Lane, the Senate, as in Committee of the Whole, proceeded to consider House bill, No. 1044, for the relief of John Gray. The bill directs the Commissioners of Pensions to place the name of John Gray, of Noble county, Ohio, upon the pension roll, and that there be paid him the sum of five hundred dollars, payable semi-annually during his natural life, commencing on July 1, 1866.

Mr. Lane said " the bill, as it passed the House, was wrongfully drawn. I move to amend it by striking out the words 'Commissioner of Pensions,' and insert Secretary of the Interior, so as to make it conform to our legislation." The amendment was agreed to. (See Congressional Globe, 2d session, 39th Congress, page 1309, et. seq.)

The bill was reported to the Senate as amended; the amendment concurred in, and ordered to be engrossed and read a third time. The bill was then read a third time and passed.

On the 15th of February, 1867, the bill as amended and passed in the Senate was sent to the House, where, on the motion of Mr. Price, the amendment of the Senate was concurred in. (See Congressional Globe, 2d session 39th Congress, pages 1262 and 1275.

A motion to reconsider the vote concurring in the Senate amendment was laid on the table, and a message sent to the Senate, announcing that the House had passed bill No. 1044, for the relief of John Gray, a Revolutionary soldier.

In the House of Representatives, on the 16th of February, 1867, Mr. Trowbridge, from the Committee on Enrolled Bills, reported that the committee had found, upon examination, bill No. 1044, for the relief of John Gray, a Revolutionary soldier, truly enrolled by its proper title, whereupon the Speaker signed the same. (See Congressional Globe, 2d session, 39th Congress, page 1285.)

On the same day, a message was received in the Senate, announcing that the Speaker of the House of Representatives had signed the bill as engrossed, and thereupon it was signed by the President *pro tem.* of the Senate. Thus John Gray was placed on the pension roll at the rate of five hundred dollars per annum.

Two days after, February 18, 1867, Samuel Downing, of New York, was placed on the Revolutionary pension roll. From the report of the Commissioner of Pensions for the year 1867, it appears that the names of John Gray and Samuel Downing only remained upon the roll: the rest were dead. Of that noble band of patriots, they alone survived. Late in the fall of 1867, Samuel Downing died at Edinburgh, Saratoga county, New York. John Gray still lived, unquestionably the last soldier of the Revolution, till the 29th of March, 1868, when he died. The soldiers of the Revolution are extinct.

> "This was the noblest Roman of them all;
> The last of all the Romans—fare thee well."

It is time to prove the leading statement of this history, namely that John Gray was the last soldier of the Revolution. That he *was a* Revolutionary soldier is proved elsewhere in this book; but here we are to show that he was the *last* Revolutionary soldier.

I wrote to the Commissioner of Pensions at Washington, D. C., to settle this. He replied by an endorsement on my letter, stating that "John Gray, of Ohio, and Samuel Downing were the only two soldiers remaining on the pension rolls of the Revolution, and that they were both alive in September last." Then I saw there were only two left. The question came up, is Samuel Downing dead? If he is, then John Gray is the last soldier of the

Revolution, beyond a doubt. So I wrote, and received the following letter, which settles the question forever:

Post Office, Saratoga Springs,
April 16, 1868.

Sir: In answer to your letter of the 12th instant, I have to say that *Samuel Downing* died last fall at his home in Edinburgh, this county.   Yours, respectfully,

M. A. PIKE, P. M.

[Note.--It will be remembered that *John Gray died afterwards*, March 29, 1868, AND WAS THEREFORE THE LAST SURVIVOR OF THE REVOLUTION. And thus the question is settled forever.]

A bright day in June, 1867, I visited JOHN GRAY, of MOUNT VERNON, VA., for the last time. I felt a deep interest in the old hero, because I knew him long and well, but chiefly because I knew he was the last living man who could say of a truth—

"I HAVE SHAKEN HANDS WITH WASHINGTON AND FOUGHT UNDER HIM. I WAS BORN AT MOUNT VERNON AND WAS HIS WARM PERSONAL FRIEND."

I knew no mortal man except John Gray could say these words. I sought for his history. He had a history worth knowing. To fill out the volume of our Colonial and Revolutionary history only one name more was left—it was the name of John Gray, of Mount Vernon. But to get his history was no easy task. He had been a common man. His deeds were not in print. Only from his lips could I gather up the ravelled thread of his life. To him, therefore, I went, and to his neighbors; and from them gleaned the fragmentary points presented in this volume. If the reader will read as patiently as I have written, he will lay down this book satisfied that John Gray was the last survivor of Washington's army. If the reader finds any discrepancies or contradictions, let him remember that the field from which I glean is one a hundred years old, grown over thickly with the weeds of forgetfulness, and covered, for the most part, with the fog of oblivion. John Gray did not figure in public life. He was a plain man, like Lincoln. From such a life it is hard to gather strange incidents. I give the facts as I got them from time to time, from an old man, nearly in his grave. He had no writings. He had no records. And I make no comments, as is the fashion of prosy historians. I enter a new domain of history, and do not repeat the familiar story of the Revolution. You know all that history.

You can see John Gray's humble connection with great events, without putting on my glasses. So I merely drop the facts. You may elaborate. I deal with points. You may detail. I profess to tell the world a new and wonderful story of a wonderful old man. This is all I claim. I point to the evidence in the acts of Congress, and in the letter of the Governor of Ohio. A vast crowd of witnesses attest the truth of this history. The proof is plain. It is given in fragments. You can pick them out. It will interest you as story never interested you before. Such is the plan of this history of the last man of the Revolution — a plain tale of truth. If I take my own way of telling the old man's story, you cannot blame me after you have read it.

"Washington is in the clear upper sky," and John Gray, his last soldier, has joined him in the land of spirits. Sixty-eight years ago Washington died. John Gray died March 29, 1868. Washington was the first soldier of the Revolution. John Gray was the last soldier of the Revolution. The whole army had died before John Gray died. Alone John Gray remained as a venerable monument of that noble generation. Washington was a Virginian. John Gray was a Virginian, too. Washington was a patriot and a Christian; so was John Gray. Washington fought for our liberty and independence; so did John Gray. One after another the Revolutionary soldiers dropped off, until John Gray alone survived. Like the sentinel of Pompeii, John Gray remained sublimely resolute at his post of duty until God had removed all his companions in arms by death, and then he folded his hands quietly over his patriotic heart and fell asleep in Jesus, in his 105th year. Washington's home was Mount Vernon. John Gray's birth-place was Mount Vernon. It would seem as if this coincidence worked a charm to preserve John Gray alive. It would seem as if to be born at Mount Vernon were to inherit immortality, as of one bathed in the fabled stream whose waters were said to confer immortality. It seemed as if born at Mount Vernon he could not die.

And here we submit material for a grander history of John Gray; for this history is an unhewn *Boulder of Truth*.

Whoever may hereafter visit Mount Vernon, let him remember that Washington's last soldier was born upon its ample acres. Let him remember, too, that John Gray was a dear personal friend of Washington. That hand crumbling to dust in that white

...ottin there i as often pressed the hand of John Gray. Wherever hereafter you go about the dear shades of Mount Vernon, remember that John Gray's sturdy arm felled trees here, and his skilful hands helped to adorn Mount Vernon for his Chieftain's eye. Washington little thought, when last he pressed the hand of his soldier John Gray, that John Gray was to outlive him by nearly three generations, and speak his fame to another century. Washington was only thirty years older than John Gray. His chances to live as long as John Gray seemed fair and flattering. But John Gray outlived his chief well nigh three-quarters of a century. It is of this wonderful old man this book speaks. His fame should keep company with the venerable fame of Washington forever. Washington the first soldier—John Gray the last soldier. Worthy every way is John Gray of a place beside the name of Washington, for his life was pure and good. The volume of the history of the Revolution remained open till John Gray died. The volume now closes. This book finishes the history of the Revolution. Nothing more remains, but that we forever revere the memory and imitate the virtues of such men as Washington and John Gray.

Mr. Gray narrated to me the following anecdote of General Washington, in June last. I believe it has never before been published, and as it gives a new view of General Washington's characteristic kindness, it is worth preserving.

"At this time (after Mr. Gray had returned from the Continental Army) he lived near Mount Vernon. There was then a saw-mill, running by water-power, of course, on a stream called Dog Run. The General's negroes came there with whip-saws in their hands one bright May morning, and with them also came John Gray, with a whip-saw, too. Sawing was a slow business then. What could not, however, be sawed with the large saw, Mr. Gray and the slaves easily sawed with the whip-saws. As he was busily sawing one day, and musing over his Revolutionary experience, who should ride up but General Washington himself. With characteristic kindness the great man called to John Gray, for he knew him well. John dropped his saw, and in a twinkling was shaking hands with the General. The General inquired kindly for his health, and telling him not to work too hard, bade him good bye and rode away." It did me good to hear the old veteran tell it. I might fill a volume with similar anecdotes, for Mr. Gray never tired of speaking of General Washington.

EULOGY ON JOHN GRAY.

"Eulogies turn into elegies." Indeed, the eulogy and elegy come properly at one and the same time. The final judgment cannot be pronounced, either in this world or the next, until the man is dead. "Well done, good and faithful servant" has already welcomed John Gray to Heaven. The welcome of the skies may well find an echo here. A life of virtue, in its fullest sense, was the life of this grand old man. Listen. John Gray was a citizen of Ohio for threescore years and ten, and you cannot find in that State one man, woman, or child who can recall one evil word he ever said, or one bad act he ever did. Nay, more. Not one man, woman, or child in Ohio has ever so much as said that such a rumor ever was heard. This would be great praise. But we can go further. Until stricken by the infirmities of age he labored hard with his hands, and led a life of noble usefulness, prayer, and virtue. Because he was inoffensive, it does not follow that he lacked mental capacity. By no means. But he sought to do good and be good, and he accomplished it. What an example to hold out to the rising generation. This man was a patriot—he fought for your liberty. This man was a Christian during a long, long life. He never injured his neighbors in thought, word, or deed. Was he not worthy to be Washington's last soldier? He was not as great, but he was as good as Washington. And are there not purposes of God plainly seen in his life? Did God prolong John Gray's life until John Gray alone remained of all the Revolutionists, and this without a purpose? Verily, no. God had a purpose in it. Might it not be that by his pure life he might forever stand as an example to coming generations?

And has not Labor her heroes? There are heroes who marshal armies and rule nations. Are there not heroes, too, in humble life? To be good as John Gray was, and do his whole duty to his God and his fellow-man, is such heroism as stands high above that of Napoleon. Therefore, I honor John Gray. Therefore, I gather up what I can of his life and write it here, that coming generations may see and admire the pure and unpretending virtues of Washington's last soldier.

In June last, when I visited him at his home, he was sitting by the fireside. The day was hot, but the old man had quite a fire burning, and he sat up close to it, for, as I have elsewhere said,

"His blood had lost the fervor
Of a hundred years ago."

I came in. The old man looked up, and hardly knew me at first. My friend, Matthew McClary, Esq., called to the old man, and told him who I was. Instantly he recognized me, and reached out that hand which had so often grasped the hand of Washington. I seized his hand and kissed it, and felt that I was blessed to have the privilege. The old man's hearing was quite dull, and his eyesight very dim. But he could both see and hear a little. He told me he was five feet eight inches high, though as he sat doubled up in an old man's way, he appeared much shorter. He was grown heavy, but by no means corpulent. He laughed as I remarked that he was not much fatter than he was the last time I had met him. "O, no," said he, laughingly, "we old men don't fatten much on hog and hominy, and the poor tobacco we get now-a-days." He had a large spittoon by his side, a wooden box that would hold half a bushel—contents thereof better imagined than described. But we pass it by with a forgiving smile. It was his only fault. He had chewed tobacco for about a hundred years, and could not leave it off.

THE ARMY IN HEAVEN.

The Army in Heaven to-night,
With garments twice covered with blood,
Once washed by the dear Crucified,
Once rolled in the battle's red flood ;
The Army in Heaven to-night
Are calling to us o'er the wave,
And bidding us stand for the Right
Till we triumph like they o'er the grave.

Over our flag they are keeping
As faithful a guard as of yore ;
No sentinel spirit is sleeping
That pickets the line of the shore ;
The voices of music are ringing,
And anthems are gushing abroad—
The Army in Heaven are singing
The praise of America's God.

The River of Death intervenes
Between us and angels to-night;
We dwell in humanity's scenes,
They soar up in heaven's pure light.
The sentinels pacing each side
Of that dark and fathomless stream.
Conversing as sweet o'er the tide
As Heaven and earth in a dream.

J. M. DALZELL.

Mr. Gray's religious principles were firm and immovable. But he was not one to accept a dogma or creed without a good reason therefor. In his earlier years he had some doubts as to the truth and inspiration of the Bible. But upon examination his reason was fully satisfied of its blessed truth, and his heart fully converted to its holy teachings. He told me that in his boyhood he read the quibbles of the infidel Paine, whom he had often seen. "You know," said he to me, "St. Luke asserts that Jesus ascended to heaven from Bethany, and St. Matthew says that it was from Galilee, and there are also some other things hard to reconcile. But of the truth of the Bible I now have no doubt. Passages there are which I cannot explain or understand, but there is enough for me that I can understand. I know that 'my Redeemer liveth.' I know that Christ died for me, and that through Him I hope for life eternal; and that makes me happy, and is enough for me. I can't explain everything in the Bible. Neither can I explain how corn grows. No man can. But I can understand enough of the Bible that is plain. I know corn grows, even if I can't tell how it grows. I know the sun shines, but I don't know what it is made of. These hard things I leave to wise men. I have not much learning. Bless God! I can read the Bible, and understand what I must do to be saved. That is enough. It makes me happy. God has been good to me. I love Him, and try to serve Him, and hope to see Him yet in heaven. That is my religion." And in that religion John Gray lived and died.

Let it be borne in mind that John Gray was not illiterate. His parents were poor, and lived with much difficulty by their daily labor; but they took pains to give John the best education at their command. John could read and write when he went into the army. He said about the greatest pleasure he had while in the army was in writing home to his poor old widowed mother. He told me that he went to school two winters to Joseph Ross, a gentleman who kept school at his own house, about four miles from where John lived. He used to be up bright and early, chop wood, kindle the fires, feed the stock, and be off on his four miles of a morning walk to school, before seven o'clock in the winter time. Little did he or his teacher then think that these humble studies he then pursued were to be useful to him for well nigh a hundred years of after life. Certain it is, that, for the last ninety years of John Gray's life, the little reading and writing which he learned of Joseph Ross were John Gray's greatest comforts. He read but few books, but with great care, and remembered almost every word. The Bible, Pilgrim's Progress, The Plain Man's Pathway, and the Constitution, he could repeat off the book, almost word for word.

His want of property excluded him from voting in Virginia for his beloved Washington. And he often said, had it not been for that, he might have lived and died in Virginia. But he was a Republican at heart, and could not well get over the insult thus levelled by aristocratic distinctions against his proud manhood. Saving this, John Gray was a true lover of Virginia. He often mourned and even wept over Virginia's wayward course in the Rebellion—for John Gray was loyal; but when the war was over all his feeling against Virginia left him. He remembered that Washington and he were born in Virginia, had fought a common foe in Virginia, and had returned in triumph from a war that closed so grandly in Virginia. No Virginian need ever blush to acknowledge John Gray's fame. He was a true Virginian, proud of the Old Dominion—with all her faults loving her still.

I asked him last June if he would hang Jeff. Davis. "O, no," said the old man, "that would do no good. The war is over. It would only raise bad feelings against us. He can't do us any harm. Let him live." I asked him if he thought the South would come back all right. "O, yes, I guess so," responded the old soldier, "when she cools off a little. You know those Southern folks are pretty hot-blooded; but they'll come around all right by and by." I asked his opinion of Grant. "Well," said he, musingly, "he is a great General; but I can't see into him very well. But he will be our next President, though."

JOHN GRAY'S IDEA OF WAR.

In my conversations with the last soldier of the Revolution, I was careful to get his opinions upon all kinds of subjects. He thought deeply and spoke slowly at first, but kindling with his subject, he would sometimes pour forth torrents of eloquence— never shall I forget his earnest manner as he spoke to me about war. He had been a soldier for his country. Of this he was grandly proud. He had been one of Washington's favorite soldiers. Of this he was doubly proud. His eyes had first opened to see the light of day near Mount Vernon, Va. As the old man recalled his memories of the Revolution, its hardships and trials, his bosom swelled, his eyes filled, and his voice trembled with emotion. O, how he loved Washington! The name was music to John Gray. He had never got done speaking of Washington, and Mount Vernon was dear to him. Often did he wish he might once more see his own dear Mount Vernon, the home of his honored General. Washington was well when John Gray left Mount Vernon. Sixty-eight years afterwards John Gray was still living, but Washington had been in heaven sixty-eight years. It seems like a miracle, but it is all true. But I was speaking of John Gray's idea of war. He detested war, except in defence of our flag; he knew what war was. I cannot better give you John Gray's idea of war than by quoting the following from him, nearly as he uttered it to me:

Here is John Gray's idea of war—

"The muses crown the gory head of Mars with gay fantastic laurels; the graces follow in his train; the Fauni come leaping from the woods, and the Nereids dancing from the waters, and all the arts of poesy, painting, and sculpture, combine their magic efforts to adorn his bloody temple, into which the millions of a continent are crowding to do him homage.

"The new Juggernaut is hailed with more than Hindoo pride and enthusiasm by prostrate millions.

"Up go the shouts, and songs, and incense from the altars of the great temple, where thousands are daily immolated, and on rolls the relentless car, while the people dance and shout, and the victims die.

"Poetry ought to be true, humane and rational, to be beautiful. We may, however, admire the rhythm and pathos of the poetry without approving those things it celebrates. The poet may describe well what he detests at heart, and so I think of all this fine writing, and fine singing, and fine talking about war. War is cruel, and repulsive, and hideous, and yet we admire it; we glory in it. To have killed a man in time of peace brands one with the mark of Cain forever; but in time of war, the man who kills or attempts to kill is held up as a paragon of all good. Use what pretty words you please to express it, but we are become a nation of assassins. Blood used to make the beholder shudder and shrink away ; but now the more that he sees shed the more he is pleased. It provokes a song, a great picture, or a speech, to do it honor. Implements of war are more highly honored by us than the most sacred elements of the sacraments. A cannon outshines a Bible ; the 'school of the battalion' laughs at the universities ; the implements of the agriculturalist are deemed useless and fit only to be handled by old women and cowards, and the ' councils of war ' sneer at the councils of law and religion. The common citizen of yesterday is the strutting tyrant of to-day, and the one time independent man is his involuntary slave. The law of the Medes and Persians was not more irrevocable and relentless than the thoughtless edicts of the man of ' brief authority ' who glories in his rank. The humble soldier has no right that an officer is bound to respect, while the officer can give no command that the private is not bound to obey. An officer is as sinless as Jesus, and a common soldier as fallible as Adam. Rank is everything. You must wait till you receive its commands, as if you were a condemned galley slave.

"The 'Grand Lama,' or the Emperor of China are not more absolute tyrants than many who wear the uniform of officers in the army. Crowd men together, and vice will as surely be the result as that this massing of mixed classes in an unwholesome place will produce disease.

" Language becomes polluted as well as thought and action. It is the devil's rarest, choicest school. If you doubt me, go and stay as long among the soldiers as I was, and you will not quarrel with me for all this plain truthing. And yet you praise war, the cloud of battle. And the figures of contending men look well on paper.

"You cannot hear the groans, and the thunder of battle is far from your hearing. The wounded dying uncared for ; the hungry, weary thousands lying in the snow ; the groans and cries of strong men, who never murmur till the agony of disease or wounds makes them cry aloud. Are all these pretty, fascinating things to contemplate ?

"The soldiers in the field only laugh, as I well know, at the thought that such pictures are beautiful, and while they see through all the hollow poetry of the war, they only take a simple prose view of it."

OUR FATHERS WERE ON THE RIGHT SIDE.

As our young world grows older,
And wiser, and better with time,
So men, with the care of a miser,
Will hoard up their glory sublime:
    Forth to their children showing
    Its beauty and honor, and pride,
    The patriot pages still glowing,
    "OUR FATHERS WERE ON THE RIGHT SIDE.

Heroes will haste to the altar,
And swear the American youth,
Firm as the base of Gibraltar,
To stand for the cause of the truth.
    Tide of secession still beating,
    Shall find them too strong for the tide.
    Lips with a quiver repeating,
    "Our fathers were on the right side.

CUMBERLAND, O., *April* 8, 1868.

J. M. DALZELL:

Dear Sir—You have doubtless heard ere this of the *death of John Gray.* He died Sabbath eve, March 29th, aged 104 years, 2 months and 23 days. I have his photograph and autograph copyrighted; they will be ready for delivery soon. I want you to send me the *precise* date of the act of Congress making him a pensioner, as I wish to place a few items of the old man's history on the back of the pictures. How would you like to secure a picture of the Gray residence for your history? Please reply by return mail.   Yours, truly,

I. N. KNOWLTON.

HIRAMSBURG, NOBLE COUNTY, O., *April* 1, 1868.

MR. JAMES DALZELL:

Dear Friend: The last Revolutionary Hero is gone. Those eyes that saw the infant colonies engaged in deadly conflict with the mother country are now closed. The tongue that helped to swell the notes of victory is now dumb. The heart that for more than one hundred and four years kept the blood coursing through the veins has ceased to beat—John Gray is dead. Sunday, March 29, A. D. 1868, at fifteen minutes before nine o'clock, the spirit took its flight. The mortal remains now repose in the family vault.

I take the liberty of writing to you to inform you of his death, knowing that you have felt a great interest in the old hero.

I am sorry to inform you, and I know that you will be sorry to hear, of the death of Dr. N. P. Cope. He was buried on the 12th of March last.

These things speak for themselves. I will make no comments.

We have had no mail to pass through here for the last ten days. You will see the difficulties under which we are laboring, but I suppose we cannot look for any change for the better for the next four years. Truly, yours,

P. BURLINGAME, P. M.

[Paraphrased from the Constitutional Union, Mr. Florence's paper.]

BIRTHDAY ODE ON THE LAST SOLDIER OF THE REVOLUTION.

Nearly a hundred years ago—
A hundred years to-day,
Our fathers met the British foe,
In that immortal fray,
At Yorktown then old John Gray stood,
Gave Britain her last blow,
And struck to drive the British off,
A hundred years ago.

Nearly a hundred years ago,
Our hero in his prime;
But now his head is white as snow,
His limbs grown weak with time:
But let us gather round John Gray,
The last man now alive,
And not forget this glorious day
Makes him one hundred and five.

January 6, 1868.   JAMES M. DALZELL.

HIRAMSBURGH, OHIO, *February 1, 1868.*

MR. J. M. DALZELL, *Washington, D. C.:*

Well do I remember what you have done to make old John Gray's name and fame known to the world. When you were living here, I remember that you did all you could to stir our people up to do something for the old man, in his poverty and his old age. John Gray speaks of it kindly, and remembers you for it. Last Saturday I went over—you know it is only a little way from here—and saw him. I read him Mr. Jackson's poem, and your poems too. He liked them very much. He says, as indeed all our people do, that you deserve to be remembered with a kindly remembrance, at least, for interesting yourself so much for him, in spreading his fame abroad throughout the land. The old man is a little ambitious. He is proud of being the last man of the Revolution. When he heard of Mr. Downing's death he shed tears. "Ah," said he, "we two only remained. Now Mr. Downing is dead. And as the prophet said once, well may I say now, 'I only am left,'" and the old man wept. His mind wanders a little at times, and he often imagines himself talking to the "Ginral," as he always calls Washington. Alas, he will soon talk with Washington "in the clear, upper sky." Mr. Gray's dog still guards the old man's chair. The old man still chews as much tobacco as ever. I believe he could not live without his tobacco. Just think of a man chewing tobacco for a century? It is the only fault the old man has. We all love him. Thanks to the 39th Congress, and to Judge Bingham, especially, the old man has a good pension. He wants you to write his history when he is gone. Will you do it? I know you will find it a hard job, for the old man's life has been very quiet.

Yours, truly,   N. P. COPE, M. D.

NOTE.—Doctor Cope has since died. *Sic transit gloria mundi.*

Mr. Gray was very fond of dogs. He said he had always owned a dog or two. "Though," said he, with a merry laugh, "I sometimes have had nothing else but a dog;" and musing a moment he added, "a plug of tobacco, of course, for without a dog or tobacco I should feel lost." A little white dog lay coiled up near his chair. "What is the name of your dog, Mr. Gray," I inquired. "Nice," responded he; "is not that a *nice* name," he naively inquired, while his sides shook at the witticism. He told me the biographies of several of his canine friends. I remember one only. When Mr. Gray's father first went into the army, John was but thirteen years of age; but being the eldest of eight children, the care of the family devolved upon him. They had no meat. They had nothing but a little cornmeal—rather a spare larder, my fair reader of the nineteenth century's fulness. So John went out and caught rabbits to feed the family. His dog "Lade" always was his companion upon these expeditions. What John's gun failed to bring down, Lade's flying feet soon brought low. I am glad that Mr. Gray has left us a picture of Lade. She was a red female hound, with a white ring around her neck. He told me that he never cried harder than he did the day he last saw Lade, except when he was leaving home to enter the Continental army. He told me that she died old and full of years, and he laid her down gently to sleep in the deep recesses of the woods of Mount Vernon.

LINES ADDRESSED TO JOHN GRAY.

The frosts of five score,
And many years more,
  Have whitened your blessed old hair:
Of glory a crown,
By Heaven sent down,
  Now, father, you solemnly wear.

O, this is a crown,
By Heaven sent down,
  More beautiful far than a king's:
For angels in glory
Have made it so hoary,
  And kissed all its silvery strings

Then wear the white crown
By Heaven sent down,
  For your feet shall soon press the bright shore
When yonder in glory
Your hair no more hoary,
  Will wave in the skies evermore.

O, fair is the crown
By Heaven sent down,
  For righteous old fathers in age :
A promised reward
From hands of the Lord,
  Laid down in the Bible's sweet page.

February 22, 1868.   JAMES M. DALZELL.

OFFICE OF CHIEF CONTRACTOR,
St. Louis, Vandalia, and Terre Haute Railroad,
St. Louis, Mo., *February* 10, 1868.

My Dear Dalzell: Recollecting with unaffected pleasure the many intellectual bouts we have had, and preserving a lively recollection of a few of your amusing idiosyncracies, such as "no man who wears a good coat and is educated can be hung in the United States;" and "the rising young man of the present generation conceals his drinking from the public eye, while the '*old stager*' drinks all around the circle, and a nation jokes about it." "*It's a queer way they have.*" I am to-day forcibly reminded of your enthusiastic admiration for "*Old John Gray,*" by seeing a notice of that veteran pensioner in the *Cincinnati Commercial*, of the 8th inst. I grieve to add that my memory always has been *painfully* impressed, when it recurs to the "*bouts*" above referred to. Let me, in calling your attention to a bad habit of "Old John Gray"—viz: tobacco-chewing—ask you to draw therefrom a useful lesson. He *chewed tobacco*, and now at the premature age of 104 years, is about to sink into an early grave. How deep and yet unavailing must his remorse be? Take warning! My dear fellow, 'tis nine months (by the clock) since we parted, and I trust in that period that your happiness has been uninterrupted and your prosperity unbroken. May Fortune and Fame smile upon your future. Permit me to send this under cover to Charlie, and believe me to be really and truly, now and ever,

Abstemiously, your friend,
C. W. GARDINER.

The notice referred to above is as follows :

The "last man" of the Revolutionary War is John Gray, who lives with his step-daughter, Mrs. McElroy, in Brookfield township, Noble county, Ohio. He is 104 years of age, having been born in Virginia, a few miles from Mount Vernon, January 6, 1764. He was at the siege of Yorktown when in his 18th year, but never obtained a pension until a year or two since, when it was granted to him by a special act of Congress, through the efforts of Hon. John A. Bingham. He is now nearly helpless, his hearing bad, and his eyesight nearly gone, yet he can walk on crutches. He has been a great tobacco-chewer all his life, to which his premature decay is probably attributable.

From the WAVERLEY, of December, 1866.

THE LAST MAN OF THE REVOLUTION.

By the report of the Commissioner of Pensions, but one of the Revolutionists is now living. The immortal army of Washington, all but one solitary veteran, has gone to the grave! The honor of the old guard has been sung by more than two billions of human tongues that long since have gone to the dust. And yet this old hero lives on to hear a new billion of tongues trumpeting the fame of the army of which he is the only living representative. In the third generation he is still living to see the glory which Washington and his comrades achieved by valor and patience. But the writer knows of one Revolutionary soldier whose name was never on the pension rolls of the United States: John Gray, now 103 years of age, who resides with his daughter, in Noble county, Ohio. He was born at Mount Vernon, Virginia, January 6, 1764. He was but a mere boy when the war began, and his father being in the army, he, the oldest of eight children, remained at home to help support the family. He says that he and his brother would go to the forest and fields to catch rabbits, and that was all the meat they had. At one time he worked a whole week at ploughing for two bushels and one-half of corn. His father fell at White Plains, and he, then only about 16 years of age, promptly volunteered, took up the musket that had fallen from his father's hands, and carried it until the war was over. He was in a skirmish at Williamsburgh, and was one of the one hundred and fifty men on that dangerous but successful expedition of Major Ramsay.

He was mustered out at Richmond, Virginia, at the close of the war, and returned to field labor near Mount Vernon. Mr. Gray married twice in Virginia, and once in Ohio. He survived his three wives and all his children, except one daughter, who is now nearly eighty years of age, and with whom he resides in Noble county, Ohio.

He has always been a poor man and a Christian. He never attempted any kind of speculation or business; but has literally earned his bread by the labor of his hands as a farmer all his life. For seventy-eight years he has been a consistent member of the Methodist Church, and never missed a single Sabbath from church when it was possible to attend. He joined church at twenty-five. He has lived a sober, regular, and industrious life; insomuch that he is now, and has been for half a century and more, a model of

piety to his church in a degree not excelled by any of his brethren
in Christ. His hours of rising, working, and sleeping are regular
as the clock. He retires early, and rises before the sun. Seldom
is any Christian permitted so long and so well to be a "living
epistle, known and read of all men." More than threescore and
ten years has he lived to adorn the doctrine of the Saviour, by a
daily walk with God. Schooled as he was in that pure and honest
school which made Washington a good man, learning his lessons
from the fathers of the church and State who formed that beautiful system of government under which we live, John Gray has
ever been a model man. Not one man ever was heard to doubt
John Gray's sincerity as a Christian and as a patriot. On visiting
the old man recently he said to us, in reply to the question "why
he enlisted so young," "I lived and was born near Mount Vernon, the home of Washington; how could I do otherwise?" Such
an answer speaks volumes for the old patriot.

James M. Dalzell.

In a conversation with Mr. Gray one was often surprised at his
wonderful powers of description. We shall have occasion more
than once to notice this in the course of his history. He was a
great admirer of Mr. Lincoln, and in speaking of him often became eloquent. We have room for only one of these fine passages.
The following is substantially as it fell from the old man's lips,
and in point of truth and beauty is the finest eulogy we ever read.
It is doubtful if a finer passage occurs in the works of any living
man. Here is Lincoln's eulogy by John Gray, only slightly
changed:

Where the clear waters of the Shenandoah join the turbid
current of the Potomac, are three great peaks of the Blue Ridge
Mountains; three mighty granite columns, from whose lofty
summits the eye can see an area of more than three thousand
square miles of mountain, plain and valley. These three spurs of
the Blue Ridge are Bolivar Heights, Loudon Heights, and Maryland Heights.

Approach the traveller as he stands upon the bridge below, and
ask him which he deems the greatest of the three, and he will tell
you that in height, breadth, and all mountain majesty, the
heights of Maryland leads off the palm of superiority over its
other mighty brothers. Ascend Maryland Heights, and look up
the Valley of the Shenandoah, or the beautiful Valley of the
Cumberland, and from this height you can see further than from

London or Bolivar. And after you have turned your eyes back upon Maryland Heights, and gone twenty miles away, still it looms up in full view high above Bolivar or London. Bolivar is grand, London is beautiful, but Maryland is sublime. The sunshine of summer, the rain of autumn, and the frost of winter have pressed against its granite brow for sixty centuries, and yet it stands firm, unchanged, and full of grandeur as when it rolled out of the smooth right hand of God. Emblem of beauty and sublimity, an everlasting monument of Almighty power and wisdom. The lightnings of heaven have spent their fiery passions in fruitless rage against its flinty brow, and the iron hail of battle has been shattered often against its rocky breast, but still it stands mocking the artillery of heaven and earth, frowning grandly evermore at all the chance and change of its servant, Time. Twin brother with Eternity, unchanged and unchangeable, there it shall stand forever. How this mountain came to be here, we cannot tell, for we were not present when the foundations of the earth were laid; how long it shall stand, we cannot tell, for we have no access to the counsels of the Eternal. Enough to know that there stands the lofty mountain peak, lifting its rocky crest high up into the blue sky, away up to the region of the clouds, crowned with garments of sublimity, and mute and solemn as eternity.

At the commencement of this decade, three of the most prominent public men, perhaps, were Abraham Lincoln, Stephen A. Douglas, and Jefferson Davis. The name of Jefferson Davis is mentioned here, perhaps, not in good taste, but with a view to contrast the fair fame of Lincoln and Douglas with the black damnation of Jeff. Davis.

Davis was before the people for office. The Charleston convention was a failure, and Davis, determined rather to reign in the Confederacy than to serve in the Union, became the chief conspirator—the President of the Confederate States. The great heart of Douglas was broken by defeat, and he died of disappointed ambition. Lincoln outlived the war. So did Davis. Lincoln fell a martyr; Davis lives in dread of the rope of the traitor; lives with the deep curses of a nation on his head, and in his dreams is forever haunted with the gibbering ghosts of his victims, and lives on in torture looking forward to a death on the scaffold as a traitor. But high above the names of Douglas and Davis, as

Maryland above Bolivar and London, stands the immortal name of *Lincoln*.

Pure as snow is the character of Abraham Lincoln. The nations revere him as their benefactor. The poor black man, as he prays daily to the Eternal Father of us all, prays that God may make him as good as Lincoln. Lincoln was the redeemer of the negro; Lincoln is deified in the negro's soul, for did he not break off his chains and set him free?

Accustomed as we are to try to account for the final causes of every great man's success, we naturally ask how did Abraham Lincoln attain that high position among men? We shall seek in vain for a satisfactory answer. He was great. He made for himself a name that shall never die. How he did it we cannot tell. The sibyl of fate has the secret in her own keeping, and her dumb lips will never open to tell us how the destinies of Abraham Lincoln were shaped to make him what he was.

A book might be written on the schools and schoolmasters of Abraham Lincoln. It almost moves a smile to speak of his schools and schoolmasters. His biographers tell us that he never went to school more than twelve months in his life. His advantages were small for gaining book learning. In fact, he never knew much about books, that is the most of books. In the school of experience, and not in academic schools was this mighty genius reared. Genius Lincoln undoubtedly had. It was not the genius that can write an Iliad, or Æneid, or Paradise Lost; it was not a genius, perhaps, that could invent like that of Franklin, or Morse, or Fulton; it was not a genius like that of Napoleon or Grant, but it was a greater genius than any of these; at least so it seems, loved and worshipped almost as Lincoln is above all who have lived or died.

He knew more of men than of books. Webster and Sumner — Calhoun and Davis were masters of arts — but Lincoln master of hearts. The learned and erudite teachings of the schools were mysteries to Lincoln. He never translated Thucydides, or Tertullian, Homer, or Virgil — he knew nothing of fluxions or equations. Lincoln was no scholar — he might have been a great one — but of books he was indeed ignorant.

But how high does his name loom above those of Webster and Sumner, of Calhoun and Davis. They knew more of books. They were great scholars. He knew more of men. He was more earnest, more honest and persistent in his opinions. He read the great rough heart of the American people till he could repeat it easily. He sympathized with the poor, for he was poor. He sympathized with the oppressed, for he was oppressed. He sympathized with the ignorant, for he was ignorant. He had thought deeply. Just as soon as he learned anything he put it into instant practice. He did not theorize and dream. He was neither poet nor philosopher. He knew nothing of the rhetorician's rules, but he knew how to talk plainly, and sometimes with wonderful effect, as witness his great short speech at Gettysburg. He hardly ever trimmed up his speeches and rounded off his periods. He was no orator, as Charles Sumner is—but he was greater. He saw all that was in a question—dug down to the roots of things, and applied common sense to the explanation. He cared for Truth and Justice. He was a Republican from his heart. He loved men, even as a man loves the woman of his choice. He would do anything he could for the poor. He loved mercy. God made him so. He followed these natural instincts when he spoke against slavery. He hated wrong. He tried to make wrong appear wrong, and right appear right. This inherent love of right came from God—and it was the strongest power in Abraham Lincoln, for he was thrice armed, having his quarrel just. He had no care for forms or formality. It was little matter to him about ornaments, either in clothes or speech. He was a plain man—so plain people loved him. He was an humble man—so humble people loved him. He was a poor man—so poor people loved him. He was a friend of the downtrodden and they loved him. He was loyal to his heart's core—so his loyal countrymen loved him. He dived to the bottom of the questions of the day, and the people loved to hear his wisdom and behold his familiar look. He never could "put on airs." The words of his lips were "like apples of gold"—all precious, and therefore beautiful. He was too busy to trifle with men. He was honest and feared God. He never said fine speeches. He acted and talked the same way. He spoke to one poor man, in his office at Springfield, just the same as to ten thousand poor men in a crowd, or to the richest in the land at the White House. He only had one face—it was a plain one. He had been brought up poor. He had mingled with the poor. He thus learned his lessons from the poor. He raised himself up by dint of studying human nature—human wants—

human necessities, and adapting himself to them. If a man wanted to know Abraham Lincoln's views on the slavery question, if he would listen he would soon be told. He used parables as Jesus did. This made his style simple and plain. This made his words go home to the people's hearts. They understood him, and he understood them altogether. There was no double-dealing. What Mr. Lincoln learned from books never made him pedantic. He seldom went to Virgil or Horace; to Tupper or Tennyson. He had plainer and better words than theirs, and so he used his own words. His college had a large faculty. Every man he met taught him. In school he learned of Dorsey, the country school-teacher. At the grave of his mother the poor old illiterate preacher taught him. At the legislature Trumbull taught him, and Douglas taught him on the stump; of everybody and everything he learned, and then he turned around and taught the whole world, by example and precept, a lesson that they had never known, at least never so fully practiced before.

"And so I close as I began," said Mr. Gray, "the three mountain peaks of Maryland, Bolivar, and London, shall stand together forever in mute and solemn majesty, and even so the three names of Lincoln, Davis, and Douglas, close together, shall endure through all the coming ages, high above all men of these times. But high up in the blue sky of an everlasting and glorious fame, infinitely above the majesty of Douglas, and the infamy of Davis, will ever stand the peerless name of the Martyr President, Abraham Lincoln."

From the Noble County (Ohio) Republican, of May, 1867.

OLD JOHN GRAY'S PENSION AS A REVOLUTIONARY SOLDIER.

Wm. H. Frazier, Esq., of this place, received on Saturday evening last, the Pension Certificate of Old John Gray, the old Revolutionary soldier, 103 years of age, and who resides in Brookfield township, Noble (this) county. Congress passed a special act, February 22, 1866, giving him a pension of $500 per annum, to be paid semi-annually; said act taking effect July 1, 1866. When he receives this money, it will be the first he has ever received from the Government which he so long and faithfully served, since he received his last pay under General Washington.

We hope that the old veteran may yet live to enjoy many payments of the bounty that has been provided for him by Congress, through the kind interposition of our noble representative, Hon. John A. Bingham, of Ohio. The old man greatly needed this bounty. The people with whom he lives are very poor, and now that Mr. Gray's health is declining he is quite a charge upon them. The pension will be no less welcome to these poor people than to poor old John himself. It will come like a welcome blessing from heaven to their poor cabin. The Bible promises to the righteous are herein verified: "When father and mother leave thee the Lord will take thee up." "Lo I am with you always." "I will never leave thee nor forsake thee." Truly, it would be a pitiful commentary on public justice, if Washington's last soldier should be left to starve in the United States. His pension came late, but, thank God! not too late.

From the Ohio Republican, of March, 1867.

THE LAST MAN OF THE REVOLUTION.

In the chill and snow of winter,
A dark and bitter night,
While the wind is mourning sadly,
Like a lone and ruined sprite,
In a cottage in Ohio
A poor and lonely man
Sits counting o'er the hundred years
Since first his life began.

In that cabin is one window
With many a broken pane,
Through which the snow keeps drifting
With all its might and main:
And the old man sits and shivers,
For his fire is very low,
And his blood has lost the fervor
Of a hundred years ago.

His grey head bows in sadness,
His prayer is murmured low,
But God can hear him now as well
As a hundred years ago.

Call the roll of the noble old heroes
Who battled at Washington's side,
And only this voice in the cabin
Will answer—for all the rest died;
In poverty, sick, in distress, and alone,
Forgotten, neglected, yet he
Adores the fair banner he fought for of yore,
And prays for the "Flag of the Free."

J. M. DALZELL.

Meagre as it is, what I give of John Gray's history is all that can ever be stated with truth by any man, although poets, historians, and novelists will repeat my story through all coming ages.

My last visit to Mr. Gray, as before intimated, was in June, 1867. At this interview I was determined, if possible, to get more definite information in regard to his parentage and early life. My friend Matthew McClary, of Noble county, Ohio, was with me. I transcribe the notes which I then and there made of that interview. I am sorry I could not make them more full and accurate. Let future historians do so. It is my duty to give these facts just as John Gray gave them to me, without addition. Mr. Gray had grown quite infirm, and could hardly hear us speaking. His memory, of course, had somewhat failed. So this may account for some discrepancies in this book. I will not try to explain them. In the main they are not such as to give the reader any trouble, satisfied as his mind must now be of the general truth of my story. So here are the fragmentary facts elicited by that last interview. Mr. Gray's father enlisted in 1777, and fell at White Plains. Mr. Gray belonged to the militia under Captain Sanford, and they were called out in the fall, in October prior to the year the war closed.

I now give his words: "I was a mighty tough kind of a boy in them days, I tell you. I saw big, heavy men give out, but I never lagged a foot behind. We started from Fairfax C. H. and went to Fredericksburg, and from there to Yorktown. When we were near Williamsburg orders came to send out a scouting party to feel of the British, who were then trying to come up to Williamsburg. We were too weak to fight them. But our captain called for volunteers to go out on a *skrimmage*, and I volunteered with sixty others. We had gone only two or three miles when we came upon the red-coats, in large force. Just as we got near enough to fire I could see day-break. It was pretty hot for a little while, I tell you. They had cannon—we had none. They fired grape shot at us; but it was on rising ground, and they fired over us. But we had to fall back, and so we then marched to Richmond. In the next year Cornwallis surrendered. Our time was out the day we came in sight of Yorktown. I went back to hard work near Mount Vernon when the war was over. My people was mighty poor, and there was a big family of us; so as I was the oldest of a large family, I had to go to work to support them. There was eight children of us. I used to take my dog and go out and catch rabbits. It was about all we had to eat sometimes. I was married to Nancy Dowell when I was twenty years old. I first moved to Morgantown, Virginia. We had all our things in a wagon. I took a notion I would go down to Kentucky. So I built a boat, and put my family and horses aboard, and went down as far as Dilly's Bottom. There I stopped for nine years. From there I went to Fish Creek, took a lease to clear some land, and stayed there seven years. I often came up through these parts in them days. There was a salt-lick up on Duck Creek, and we used to come up and hunt of winters. I saw Indians, a plenty of them. I remember the year of Wayne's defeat. I tell you the settlements was badly skeered then. I may have shot one or two red-skins—no matter. I was married to my second wife at the Flats of Grave Creek. Her name was Mary Ragan. I don't know where my children is now—I am afeerd they are all gone, except my step-daughter. I have my crutches and a pension to support me. I am very well satisfied. God bless Judge Bingham for getting that pension he got for me. He was always kind to me. I always voted for him, because I have always known him to be a good man. I tell you we hav'nt many more such men. He is the soldier's friend. I saw that all through the war. He is always ready to do a good turn for a soldier. No wonder the boys all like him.''

Thus closed the old man's story. There he sat alone. He had outlived his generation. His white hair, still abundant, flowing down over his bent form, made him seem a patriarchal hero. We bade him good bye.

For the guidance of future historians, who shall better perform the task of writing this old man's biography, I would refer them to Howe's history of Ohio, and also to a similar work on Virginia. Doubtless the names of some of Mr. Gray's freinds may be found there. The descendents of his early friends around Mountain Vernon, Morgantown, Wheeling, Fish Creek, Dilly's Bottom, and Flats of Grave Creek, may have some curious legends of his early life. The history of Virginia does give the names of many who knew John Gray of yore. So does the history of Ohio. To those fond of the antiquarian task of searching old chronicles, much of interest there would undoubtedly be in such researches after the early history of John Gray. Noah Zane, the Wetzels, Frakeses, Gossetts, Hipsleys, Boneys, Thrapps, Morrisons, Fosters, Knoxes, Pipers, Stonekings, Scotts, Gearys, Peterses, Goodrichs, Harmans, Wileys, Parrishes, Nobles, and a multitude of other pioneer families of Ohio, must have known John Gray. So with many old families in Virginia, much may yet be gleaned from these. I have made no researches of that kind; I have contented myself with taking the few grains of fact, and leaving others to beat the old bundles of dry straw for their amusement. I suppose John Gray knew his own history, that is, the history which I give you. One might dilate much and digress more, and paraphrase infinitely. The field is inviting, but it is left for others. Think of the events which have occurred since John Gray was born. Think of the events his life outlived. Is there not a field for comment? When Bancroft, Headley, or Motley come to write up the history of John Gray, in what stately periods, with what abundant metaphor they will recount these mighty parallelisms. It will afford them an opportunity to rewrite what everybody knows. We will not try it. Our task is to gather up here a little, there a little of John Gray's history. We are not writing an old history; we are not rehearsing American history, we are finishing the history of the revolution with the history of its last soldier. The rejected stone has become the head of the corner. One niche only remained, in that we reverently write John Gray; and thus is finished, at last, the beautiful temple of the history of the Revolution.

It may seem strange, that from the beginning, I have taken such an interest in John Gray's history, I explain this by saying that John Gray was my neighbor in Ohio for well nigh twenty years, and that I loved the old man as if he had been my father. I admired him—who could help it?—for his rare and excellent qualities of mind and heart. I loved him because he had fought for the same flag that I had, and I loved him because he was so much like Washington—plain, simple, honest, and good. I bow down not to genius and rank, I worship only the heroes of the true and the good. He was such a hero. His name should not and cannot rot in oblivion. Through all coming time his name will be named with that of Washington. I look upon him as preserved through four generations to show his children and his children's children what a noble type of men were our revolutionary fathers. He was a worthy sample of that good old stock. Ask the people of Ohio, and they will tell you there never lived in Ohio a better man than old John Gray.

In the midst of a meadow is a cabin, in front of the door is an old-fashioned well, on the hill just above, and in full view, perhaps two hundred yards off, is a little enclosure grown over with weeds, where sleep the remains of John Gray's people. As I approached the cabin, the old man's dog ran out and barked fiercely at me. As I entered the cabin, a sweet girl, of perhaps fourteen years, met me with a smile and invited me in. There before me stood John Gray on his crutches, an old, old man, the oldest I ever saw, and the most reverend. On his crutches leaning, his hair falling in snowy showers about his shoulders; his hands large, for he had lived by hard labor; his feet small as a woman's; he was five feet eight inches high, broad, very broad of chest, and with a massive head of perfect symmetry. He looked up at me with his two sweet blue eyes and smiled. He was not ugly. His smile made him look handsome; his voice trembled a little, but was pleasant; a subdued and musical treble like that of a child. I expected him to sit down exhausted; he had been moving about on his crutches, and was indeed tired. But, on sitting down, he at once began to talk to us. His dog walked around and lay down quietly beside Mr. Gray, the sentinel of the old revolutionist. Thus appeared John Gray in his 105th year, in his home in Noble county, Ohio. Doubtless artists will yet set the picture in a beautiful frame in the Capitol of the nation, and thus for the first time do honor to a POOR MAN.

[From the GUERNSEY TIMES, Ohio.]

THE LAST SOLDIER OF THE REVOLUTION.

WASHINGTON, D. C., *April* 10, 1868.

Dear Republican Friends and Brothers of the Times:

I have just learned by a private letter, from my sister, Miss M. A. Dalzell, that John Gray, the last of Washington's army, is dead. The Sixteenth Congressional District will sincerely mourn the departure of this wonderful old hero. I knew the old man well. He was born at Mt. Vernon, Va., January 6, 1764, and was in the one hundred and fifth year of age at the time of his death. His father fell at White Plains, in the Revolutionary army. Like a true patriot, John Gray took up the musket which had fallen from the hands of his father, and carried it like a hero throughout the war till the surrender of Cornwallis. He was present at that memorable event. Mr. Gray returned home to field labor after the war.

He told me himself that the first day he ever worked out was at Mount Vernon, for General Washington. Just think of that!

John Gray moved to the Territory of the Northwest soon after Wayne's defeat. He has lived in Ohio ever since, till his death. Washington was born in Virginia—"first in peace." John Gray was born in Virginia—last soldier of the Revolution. Historic honor enough for "the Old Dominion." Alas, the fair escutcheon of Virginian glory has been darkened by treason, since. John Gray belonged to the Methodist Church for eighty years—certainly the longest membership ever held in that great popular church. No one ever said a word against him. His character throughout life was as pure as that of a mortal can be. Imbued with strong religious feelings and deep patriotic instincts, he was the truest, highest type of the Christian patriot. Forgetful of self, Christ and country were all in all to him. A better, braver heart never beat. It is impossible to be extravagant in his praise. John A. Bingham, who knew him well, almost adored the glorious old hero. You remember Judge Bingham found the old man in poverty and distress, gave him money out of his private purse and procured a magnificent pension for him.

Strangely enough, on the 22d day of February, 1867, the bill was approved granting John Gray $500 per annum—a fitting tribute to the last soldier of the Revolution—on Washington's birth-day.

Herald it to the world that the last soldier of the Revolution died in Ohio. Rear a marble column to tell coming generations that John Gray, Washington's last soldier sleeps in Ohio. Men of the Sixteenth District of Ohio, aye, of the whole great Commonwealth of Ohio, bestir yourselves to honor Washington's last soldier. Strike some plan by various and early subscription to raise a marble column to his memory. Washington's last soldier died in Ohio. Governor Cox wrote me last year that he sympathized deeply with a scheme to rear a monument to John Gray's memory. All good citizens of Ohio will contribute to it. Set me down for a dollar. Are there not ten thousand other dollars?

> Let a column rise to Heaven
> Till sky and marble meet,
> And sunlight of the morning
> All its pallid beauty greet.

Yours, truly,

DALZELL.

The question may arise, have I a right to write and publish a history of John Gray. The following will settle that question in a constitutional way—for now-a-days, you know, a man must show his constitutional right to do anything he may do:

At this point it may not be amiss to look back to the first provisions made by the fathers of the Constitution for the advancement of learning in the United States.

Their intention was to begin our Government on the principle of universal human equality, and so in all things to give all men an equal chance in the race of life. This is the dominant idea of our Constitution. George Washington, Roger Sherman, Alexander Hamilton, Benjamin Franklin, James Madison, and Charles Pinckney, were all literary gentlemen, and in framing the Constitution they carefully provided for the interests of literature, not less than for the interests of commerce and civil government generally. It would have been strange indeed, if gentlemen so eminently skilled in the use of our language had neglected to make the fullest and fairest provisions for art, science, and literature. But posterity has to thank the fathers for an early and wise legislation in behalf of learning. The Constitution says but little about literature, but the little it does say is ample enough to meet the case, in all points.

The rights and privileges of authorship are strongly chalked out in the Constitution. All legislation since had on the subject has found full authority in that instrument. The Constitution recognizes no graduation of human rights other than that written by the finger of God in the heart of man. An equal chance is given to all to compete for the prizes of honor, wealth and official dignity. No caste is recognized. The pen of the poorest boy in Ohio is as free and untrammeled by any constitutional law, as is the pen of a Governor or a President. You, whoever you are, my reader, have the same right, and as much right to trace your opinions on paper as has the greatest man in America. If the people care to read your thoughts, you are at perfect liberty to publish them broad cast over the land. Your hands are not fettered. Your tongue is not tied. Your thought that is in you may be freely and fearlessly proclaimed wherever you please. This is liberty of the press. This is liberty of speech. And to oppose you by force in the exercise of this undoubted right is a crime, punishable by law. Every one knows these things are so. And they are so because our Constitution makes them so. We are not left to guess what are our rights to print and speak. Let us read the words of the Constitution itself, and see what guarantees it contrains for authors and inventors. Article first, section eight, enumerating the powers of Congress gives to that body the power " to promote the progress of science and useful arts, by securing, for LIMITED TIMES, to authors and inventors, the exclusive right to their respective writings and discoveries." Three years afterwards, at the second session of the First Congress, " an act for the encouragement of learning" was passed in conformity with the foregoing provisions of the Constitution. The sole right of publication was thereby secured to authors for fourteen years only, with a privilege of continuing for a second term of fourteen years upon certain conditions. At the same time special provisions were made to so secure the exclusive right to the author that he might proceed against and punish others printing his work without his consent. In this alone does our country differ from despotic kingdoms.

The Constitution puts no chains or fetters on any tongue or pen. The points to which your attention is called are, that the First Congress fully appreciated the interests of literature and took the first and earliest opportunity to make the most wise and liberal laws to promote and encourage all kinds of literature. The rights of citizens as such, the rights of States, too, were all provided for; but still the great absorbing interests of literature were not overlooked or passed in silence by the framers of our great organic laws. The aim was two-fold—to furnish the people with useful books, and to secure the right of selling the books to those whose brains had made them. That section of the Constitution which we have quoted, refers also to all kinds of inventions and discoveries which are of public use; but we pass them by for the present to consider the provisions made in the interests of literature alone. At present let us see what are our laws about printing and speaking.

American liberty is emphatically freedom of speech and of the press. Not only are the rights of publishing and selling the books confined to the authors, but the Constitution goes further, and leaves the field open for universal competition in the matter of originating and publishing one's thoughts. Authorship is not limited to any class of citizens: all who have the mental power and culture to do so may write and publish books, and secure to themselves alone the copy-right thereof. No class privilege in that. No monopoly in that. No man can write a book, publish it and say to you or me, "there is my book, write one at your peril; I have the right, you have not." No, sir. Brain and culture, sense and education, these are all the requirements for authorship. No man is born to it. Any one who has genius may write. No man dare stop him. That is what we mean when we say "freedom of the press." It means I have as good a right to go into print as the President has. No man has a better right to write than I have. There is and can be no monopoly of letters. No monopoly of printing or speaking is given to any American citizen. In the eighth section of the first article of the Constitution, I read these words: "No title of nobility shall be granted by the United States." That means something; I think it is like all the rest of the Constitution, plain and easy to see. It means just that, and nothing else. So then we see that we are to have no poet laureates who shall live on government salaries and government honors. An equal chance is held out to you and me to write and publish, precisely as we please, as much as any other man can. That is all of it. Away with this nonsense about Tom. Dick, or Harry having a better right to publish his opinions than you or I have. You and I are the judges of the whole matter. We will write and publish if we please, and ask no man. We run the risk. If we please to publish, no man can prohibit us from so doing.

You will observe that all citizens are perfectly equal herein. In the second section of the fourth article of the Constitution : " The citizens of each State shall be entitled to all privileges and immunities of citizens in the several States." When I want to go into print in Arkansas or Maine, in California or Texas, all I have to do is to settle these questions. 1st. Am I a citizen of any State ? 2d. Does any man in any State publish a book, a newspaper, or a speech ? If the answer to these questions is, " Yes," then all I have to do is to go on and enjoy my Constitutional right of publishing freely any opinion I may have. Of course this freedom has some restrictions, as every political privilege has. Everybody sees that. Of course, no man ought to appear in print until his education and his genius warrant it. These things need hardly be said. But yet let it be remembered, the laws of the United States do not deny to any man the right of freedom of speech and freedom, with all proper legal restraints, of the press.

It is absurd to say any man has other rights than I have. Chas. Sumner has a right to speak. So have I. Horace Greely has a right to publish a paper. So have I. I have the same right, and as much right, to speak and write as Chas. Sumner and Horace Greely. Precisely the same. Let us hear no more of this monopolizing the press in America. One has the same right another has. Let this be impressed on every mind—that no writer in America has any more privilege under our Constitution than you or I may have. We have no Princes of the Pen. We have no Dukes of the Tongue. No man has the exclusive right to speech or of printing. No, no, the field is open for all. All may enter, and contend for the honors. The people are the judges. Every candidate for literary honors will stand or fall by the amount of talent, tact, and learning that he has. No man dare to exclude him from the area. The President has no more freedom of press or freedom of speech than has

Yours, truly,

DALZELL.

[From Chronicle of April 5th, 1868.]

THE LAST SOLDIER OF THE REVOLUTION.

To the Editor of the Chronicle:

I have just learned through a private letter from Ohio, that John Gray, the last soldier of the Revolution, expired at his residence in Noble county, Ohio, on the 29th of March. I knew the old man well, having lived for nearly twenty years within sight of his house, and frequently met and conversed with him. There never lived a purer or better man. During the twenty years that I knew him, I never heard one word against his character. Greater praise than that is impossible. Every citizen of Noble county, Ohio, knew and loved the old man.

John Gray was born at Mount Vernon, January 6, 1764, and was consequently in his one hundred and fifth year when he died. He told me that he worked many a day on the Mount Vernon estate for General Washington. At sixteen years of age, John Gray entered the Continental army, and served till the close of the war for our independence. He was at the surrender of Yorktown. Mr. Gray removed to Ohio before it was a State, and remained there till his death. His history will be written, but I give these few facts as they come to my mind to-day.

Hon. John A. Bingham, of Ohio, knew old John Gray well, and did much to help the old hero in his declining years.

The last soldier of the Revolution was an earnest friend of Mr. Bingham. Mr. Bingham found the old man in very destitute circumstances a few years ago, and determined to do all he could for him. For some reason, Mr. Gray had never received any pension. So Mr. Bingham gave the old man some money to relieve his most urgent necessities, and afterward prevailed upon Congress to grant him a pension of $500 per annum. This act of generosity and patriotism to Washington's last soldier was remembered greatly by old John Gray to the last hour of his life. The people of the 16th district of Ohio will never forget it.

Yours, &c.,   J. M. D.

WASHINGTON, D. C., *April* 4, 1868.

From Soldiers' Friend.

THE BLUE AND THE GRAY.

BY JAMES M. DALZELL.

You may sing of the Blue and the Gray,
  And mingle their hues in your rhyme,
But the Blue that we wore in the fray
  Is covered with glory sublime.
    So, no more let us hear of the Gray,
      The symbol of treason and shame
    We pierced it with bullets—away!
      Or we'll pierce it with bullets again,
Then up with the Blue, and down with the Gray,
And hurrah for the Blue that won us the day!

Of the rebels who sleep in the Gray,
  Our silence is fitting alone,
We cannot afford them a bay,
  A sorrow, a tear, or a moan.
    Let oblivion seal up their graves
      Of treason, disgrace and defeat:
    Had they triumphed, the Blue had been slave
      And the Union been lost in retreat.
Then up with the Blue and down with the Gray,
And hurrah for the Blue that won us the day!

Of the rebels whom our mercy still spares
  To boast of the traitorous fray,
No boy in the Blue thinks or cares,
  For the struggle is ended to-day.
    Let them come as they promised to come,
      Under Union and Loyalty too:
    And we'll hail them with fife and with drum.
      And forget that they fired on the Blue.
Then up with the Blue and down with the Gray,
And hurrah for the Blue that won us the day.

As they carried your flag through the fray,
  Ye Northmen, ye promised the Blue
That ye'd never disgrace with the Gray
  The colors so gallant and true.
    Will ye trace on the leaves of your soul,
      The Blue and the Gray in one line,
    And mingle their hues on the scrolls
      Which glorify Victory's shrine,
And cheer for the false, and hiss at the true.
And up with the Gray and down with the Blue?

Let the traitors all go if you may,
  (Your heroes would punish the head,)
But never confound with the Gray
  The Blue, whether living or dead.
    Oh! remember the price that was paid
      The blood of the brave and the true—
    And you can never suffer to fade
      The laurels that cover the Blue.
Then up with the Blue and down with the Gray,
And hurrah for the Blue that won us the day!

From The Soldier's Friend.

THE VETERANS BEGGING.

BY JAMES M. DALZELL,
Of the One Hundred and Sixteenth Ohio Vol. Inf.

Oh! 'tis a piteous sight to see
  An aged father come
And beg for bread, and be denied
  By haughty sons at home.
Ingratitude of darkest dye,
  More piteous far than that,
To see the wounded soldier hold
  For alms his slouching hat.

Oh! see him stand for hours and days,
  Where wealth and pride are near,
Lean on his crutch, and beg for bread,
  With many a burning tear.
His proud heart pulses crimson pride
  O'er manly cheek and brow,
But hunger mutters through his soul—
  " In battle *brave, be now.*"

Again he feels the battle-shock,
  The bullets whistling by,
The whizzing shell, the blinding smoke.
  The demon rebel cry :
Again he feels, oh! ten-fold more—
  More sore because afresh—
The bullets tearing through his limbs,
  And crushing bone and flesh.

He wakes, but not a rebel yell
  Nor rebel host is there :
But Peace sits smiling on the scene,
  While Plenty hoards with care.
He feels his wounds anew again—
  O God ! can this be so ?
The soldier wounded by his friends
  As well as by the foe !

Let Peace still smile upon the scene,
  And Plenty pass him by,
And all the promised gifts of these
  Pass into *words* and die ;
But tell me not a grateful land
  Can suffer this to be,
Till every star in Freedom's Flag
  Is quenched in Treason's sea.

WASHINGTON, D. C., 1868.

INTROSPECTA.

Two pair of eyes to see,
  One pair without, and one
To scan the world within,
  By man are seldom won.

The ox has eyes to see
  The straw on which he tramps
But in that mammoth bulk
  There burn no spirit lamps.

Man alone has power to gaze—
  And few men even this—
On Beauty's charms, and feel
  Electric romance, bliss!

This is the eyne I love,
  The power to look within
To fill the empty air
  With visions bright akin.

To the higher forms and moulds
  So transubstantial broad:
The glowing bust divine
  Of Beauty, Music, God.

To hear anthems pealing
  The spirit aisles all through,
Till the heart quakes with joy,
  Stirring, sublime, and true.

I see shapes in the night
  No other eyes can see:
I hear strange voices ring
  In accents full of glee.

And pale groups of ghosts
  Around my pillow flit,
And I wake from ghostly dream,
  "To many a musing fit."

I feel the touch of hands
  No other mortals feel:
And fight, with demon arms,
  Hosts mailed in more than steel.

I talk familiar with
  The spirit of Perfect Life,
And see her footsteps strike
  From earth, its toil and strife.

I touch hands, as if friends.
    With Beauty ranging all
Nature's pure and sweet domains,
    And feel her blessings fall.

This is a high joy to me,
    And I love to live in
Creations thus illumed
    With lamps just lit in heaven.

The dusty toil and drag
    Of a weary life, and poor,
I would not lengthen out a day,
    Were I compelled to live a boor.

But sometimes it seems to me
    'Twere better I were dead,
Than drink at founts of joy
    By the heart's red current fed.

For these passion lamps must drink
    The being's ripest oil,
And end its flickerings all
    With life of aimless toil.

Burn on ye lamps within, burn
    Till ye burn the spirits down:
Then ashes fly in Fate's cold face,
    And tell her I was not a clown!

Come, ye cold eternal winds,
    And flap your wings into my face.
For sooner shall it cool not
    In time's tempestuous chase!
                    J. M. DALZELL.

WASHINGTON, D. C., *April 29*, 1868.

———◆———

Where did our Bible come from? God handed it down to his people in the country. He addressed his meek servant from a burning bush; He opened the heavens and descended in thunderings and lightnings upon trembling Sinai; He sent his people to dwell in a land flowing with milk and honey; He hid his prophet in a rock; He sent the ravens to feed another holy man; He sent Samuel to annoint a country-boy as the king of Israel; and in a thousand places, and in diverse ways showed his will and pleasure in the country. The reader of revelation need not be reminded that almost every inspired writer lived in the sacred solitudes, away from the city. Some were shepherds, some were farmers, in a certain sense; and nearly all lived in the country. And then the sweet poetry of every age; where did it spring from? As the shell sings of the sea, so genuine poetry sings of the scenes that gave it birth : and hence read your poetry, and see how much of it was produced in rural scenes. The poetry of the Bible, the sublimest songs, because from the sublimest source, the poetry of the Bible, came from the simple children of nature. Go read that first song of emancipation, sung on the bloody shores of the Red sea, after the " bubbling death groan " of the Egyptian host had died away forever : read the tender, touching story of Ruth : follow the sweet singer of Israel through his heavenly flights ; go then to the "Song of Songs," and as you read there the tender address of the Redeemer to his redeemed people, inhale that holy enthusiasm that will qualify you for joining with Isaiah, to sing strains of divine music. The Bible, the poetry of the Bible, the celestial imagery of inspiration, as if too pure and holy for the city, were first poured down in rural scenes.

Painting and sculpture were at least commenced away from the clamor and smoke of crowded cities. You can easily imagine some shepherd, sitting on a green bank, looking down into a quiet stream, and there seeing his own image reflected, starting up to make an imitation of it on some smooth rock, with his shepherd's crook : or marking with blood, or the juice of the red-mountain berries upon the great leaves that he has plucked from the palms below. And again you behold him stooping down to collect some red clay, with which he is to form a rude image of his dog or his sheep. Here may have been the commencement of those fine arts that since have engaged the genius of a Wren, a Reynolds, a Parr, and a West. In fine, we see the peasant or the shepherd at one time a philosopher, reasoning on the causes and effects of rain, sunshine and darkness ; at another, a poet singing the praises of Pad, or faithful Ceres, upon an oatstraw pipe, invoking the aid of his imaginary muse : at another time, the subject of a powerful inspiration, writing " what man is to believe concerning God, and what duty God requires of man ;" at another time we hear him uttering strange sounds, and see him writing on bark and leaves and skins, always inventing or discoursing, always beginning the work of civilization, reformation, and general education. All honor, then, to the farmer ! that he is always found in the vanguard of every noble and effective work. Just as the sons of the soil, the men of stalwart form and giant limbs are first to clear our forests and prepare our roads, they are first to polish the rude, unclassic mind, and elevate the race. He sits no longer, like the simple ancients, on towers and cliffs to catch the shadow of coming events from the flight of birds, or listen to the sound of their wings, or burning laurel, or star-gazing; but in the clear, plain sunshine of intelligence he thinks, reads, and thinks, and judges with a clear head and a pure heart. No longer does he stand, like Andromache, pouring out milk and blood on the honorary tomb of a hero, but near the real tomb of his patriot fathers he swears eternal vengeance to tyranny, and eternal allegiance to freedom. He goes to no Helicon and Parnassus to drink inspiration from fabled muses, gods, and fountains, but he hurries to Mount Vernon, the Delphian vale of America, and stands anon on Bunker Hill with enthusiasm, and a desire to make America worth the blood that was there poured out for her redemption — and to make her thus great and noble by cultivating her generous soil, and improving her extensive lands. He remembers the time when a devastating army wasted and impoverished his country so that a cartload of continental money would not buy a wisp of hay. and he determines to make his country rich and strong, so that if a warlike force should invade his land, it will have the power to repel his violence and drive him away with speed. He is an upright, honest man, the "noblest work of God," "eyes nature's walks, shoots folly as it flies, and catches the living manners as they rise." God has appointed him to be his treasurer, and he feels it!

There are persons who, as Halleck says, "Are too proud to weep," and too polite to swear, who imagine that the honors of the peasant are very humble and mean. Would such a one hear an illustration of the principle that contentment, not station, imparts happiness? A Roman general was once passing the Alps, and stopping at a little village of simple mountaineers, he was praised, and one asked him if he were not very happy. He replied, "Indeed I am not! I would rather be the chief of this village than the proudest general of Rome!"

No one knew how heavy his honors pressed upon his proud heart, as he vainly strove to satisfy that unholy ambition which is so common to the high and noble, and so seldom found among the inhabitants of the country. A certain woman observing Aristozones weaving a splendid diadem, expressed her opinion that he must be happy. "O, mother," returned he, "if you knew how I feel. If you saw a diadem lying on a dung-hill you would not pick it up." O, the simple joys of the country. How far they transcend the pleasures of the camp, the city, or the great emporiums of trade.

Survey now the history of departed ages; call the roll of the mighty dead, the dead that are yet, like Webster, living, and as you call their names, ask them where they were born, and tell me how many hoarse voices reply, in the country. Is it not a multitude that no man can number? Those who were born in the city are the exceptions! Geometry, that pure, natural science; algebra, that system of signs and symbols, and surveying, all were born in the country. The whole system of circles, curves, plains, triangles, and lines, is mapped out in the fields and on the shores of every land, and from things so simple as the curve of a river, or the angles of lands and stones, men proceeded by imitation, copying nature and reducing her laws and forms to rules and systems.

It is a matter of history, that only for the inundations of the Nile we should probably yet have to write that "Things which are equal to the same thing are equal to each other;" or that other law, that, "The square described on the hypothenuse of a right-angled triangle is equivalent to the sum of the squares described on the other two sides."

To Arabia we owe the discovery of arithmetic—to a country where towns are rare.

What in science do we not owe to the country?

But Son of Science, will you acknowledge that the simple children of nature—the peasant and the shepherd have given you your dearest themes?

You say Homer, the rich old bard of Scio's isle was a countryman. Undoubtedly he drank his inspiration from the classic shores, from the pleasant hills and vales of blooming Greece. But was not the mother of Demosthenes a root-gatherer? O what a contrast; one day to see the boy following his mother to the fields to dig herbs and roots in the hills of Greece, and another to see him standing up before thousands of his assembled countrymen, making the very throne of Philip rock and tremble. Brutus, Cincinnatus, Scipio, Cato! What a constellation of countrymen! Virgil himself cultivated a farm near Mantua, as is evident from the fact that after the lands around about that place were divided among the Roman soldiery, Virgil's lands were restored to him by Augustus. Compare Antony, raised and pampered in luxury, to plain unassuming Brutus, willing only to die for or free his country. How often is the contrast between the proud citizen and the humble peasant as great. As we pass, notice Jerome and Augustine, the sterling fathers of Christianity, and tell me did they spend their lives in bestial Rome or haughty Athens? Newton was not in a city when he discovered the law of gravitation—he was sitting in an orchard! Gassendi was travelling through the country when he proved to his boyish companions that they saw the clouds and not the moon moving. Goldsmith and Burns were nearly always in the country. Byron and Scott and Moore spent much of their time in the fields.

It seems reasonable for man communing with nature to rise in his thoughts to the Author. " If there is design, there must have been a designer ; and that designer was God." Thus, Thompson, speaking of the Seasons, says :

" These, as they change, are but the varied God.

The drift of all these remarks is to show that it requires Christianity to make even the farmer happy. I believe it is easier for the farmer to be a Christian than any other man, merely because he has fewer cares and simpler joys and less temptation. I don't believe they are the only happy men, but they are the most generally happy of any other class of men.

But, as I am to speak about the country without coloring too highly the picture of rural felicity, let us leave the poet's fiction and fancy and ask first, what do we owe to the country? We all love music. It was born among the hills and valleys. The " morning stars sang together"—" the sons of God shouted for joy." We read about " the music of the spheres," and how " when music, heavenly maid, was young, first in early Greece she sung." We have listened to the old legend that a shepherd attending his flocks on the mountains broke off a reed and was rejoiced to hear the sweet sounds he could produce upon it. Nature gave us music, but yet she retained eternal volumes of it for the country. She has placed a pipe in the mouth of every member of the feathered choir, and among the branches of her leafy children they delight to make music all the year. Break your pianos, melodeons, and dulcimers, and every stringed instrument of music, and come with me to the mountains and listen to the music of the waterfalls, and the perpetual base of the ocean below, or the deeper base of the thunders above, and the wild soprano of the winds and think you, can we not reproduce those instruments again?

The farmer searches causes and effects among the elements. He remembers the time when the sea-weed was counted useless, but now hears that iodine is useful in daguerrotyping and more useful in curing scrofula; he knows the crocus yields a most effective cure for the gout; he knows the potato in Peru was once thought useless, and he laughs as he smokes his evening pipe to read about a certain king writing a great book against tobacco; he knows the use of the twisted leaf of China, the cane of the Indies, and the fragrant gums of Arabia. All these things the true farmer knows, and by them he is encouraged to study everything and see what use it can be put to. He believes

> " That they whom truth and science lead,
> May gather honey from a weed ;"

He " reads sermons in stones, books in running brooks, good in everything." The zephyr, the harebell, the hyacinth, the rose that blooms in his garden, and the eglantine and myrtle that circle round his " old house at home ;" the thunder, the storm, the calm, the seasons, the fields—everything teaches him some useful lesson. He is a student of Nature. Only one great slur has ever been put upon the peasant. It is his want of refinement and breeding. If refinement is to dissimulate and act the hypocrite, then the farmer has not much refinement. He is usually a plain man. He tells a man he thinks that he is honest, that he is dishonest, that he is a wise man or a fool, just what he thinks, plainly. Refinement says " don't speak your mind, be cunning !"

O that those who charge clownishness and impoliteness on the peasantry, would remember the time they must spend in the sunshine and the shade, and the rough labors of the fields and forests. Fops and useless dandies in cities and towns, good for nothing and burdens to community, should never be allowed to say anything against the honest farmer.

The farmer has no time for travel and reading, says another. He has little time I admit, but in this little time his mind is fresh and clear and active, and hence we find many farmers who are well acquainted with politics, science and religion. Lord Burleigh advised his son Robert Cecil, afterward Earl of Salisbury, " Not to suffer his sons to cross the Alps, for they shall learn nothing there but pride, blasphemy, and atheism ; and if by travel they get a few broken languages, that shall profit them nothing more than to have one meat served in diverse dishes." We know this is true. How often have we seen our young men go out like the prodigal son and spend all their substance in riotous living, and then return and settle down in a rented cabin to starve themselves and families. We do not expect farmers to be travellers and readers, like Taylor and Benjamin, any more than we expect stage actors and tailors to be expert at making rails and driving oxen. "Act well your part," says some one, "for there the honor lies." Cicero affirmed that it was not the part that we have in the play, but the way that we act our part that gives us the honor.

*　　　　*　　*　　　　*　　*　　*

Slavery was the mother of treason and adultery in a thousand forms, the prolific parent, too, of rapine, murder, and a thousand forms of oppression.

Slavery ignored human rights. The cry was not against the black man alone, it was against all the poor.

Slavery loved to live in dark places, concocting and executing hellish crimes.

When the slave system was shattered to pieces with Union bullets the cry of vengeance rose from the black lips of treason as it stood shivering over the bloody remains. Then Booth fired, and Lincoln fell. Then the traitors banded together to renew the conflict. Then innocent blacks were shot and hung, and Union men murdered in their beds. Following this came the riots at the South. Then the miserable rebel governments came insolently knocking at the doors of Congress. Blatant blackguards and traitors, with hearts like devils and faces of brass, dared to parade Pennsylvania avenue in rebel uniform. They dared even to profane Independence Hall, in Philadelphia, with shouts of treason at the Convention in August. Here was born the Ku-Klux-Klan.

Alarmed at these signs of reviving treason, the friends of the country rallied once more to save the Government. Thank God, by the ballot they have succeeded well. Thanks to Boys in Blue.

The men who murdered unoffending negroes at the South, and the men who incited riots there, and the men who preached a crusade against the Thirty-Ninth Congress, called themselves

"Conservatives. A mild name, indeed, that is for men who could fire on the star-spangled banner. Conservatives—Conservatives yes, these same Conservatives fired on the flag at Fort Sumter, and never ceased their fiendish efforts to destroy the Union, till Grant compelled them at Appomattox to surrender up themselves and their arms. How were the mighty fallen then! Then they promised, aye swore to submit to the Government of the United States. How well they have kept these oaths history shall tell. Their history since 1860 will be comprised under the heads of Perjury and Treason, when the new Encyclopædia American comes out.

Grant compelled them once to surrender.

Grant will compel them to surrender again in November.

But what do you call the men who oppose all these rebels? Why, they are Union men. None of them ever fired on the flag. These men are the Republican Party, the only Union party in the land. These are the men who fought your battles at Bull Run, at Shiloh, Stone River, Antietam, Gettysburg, Atlanta, and the Wilderness. This party always said slavery was wrong. This party killed slavery. This party saved the Constitution of the United States. The Conservative party tried to destroy the Constitution. But some call the Union party Radicals. Radical indeed they are. Earnest men are always Radical. Good men are always Radical. Bad men are always Conservative. A Conservative winks at one man, and then at the other. A Radical has one face only. A Conservative has two faces, and can smile on one side, and frown on the other at the same time. A Radical believes all men have rights, and tries to secure these rights to all. A Conservative thinks Rights are all bosh, and he thinks no one but himself has rights.

A Conservative begins his prayers with "O, good God," or "Good devil." The Radical, knowing he is right, looks up manfully to God, and says "Our Father." The Conservative kisses like Judas, and denies like Peter. The Conservative trembles lest he offend somebody. The Radical knows offences will come to every one who endeavors to free and enfranchise his fellow men.

The better impulses of our nature are radical. When I see a man strike a woman or a child, I feel like knocking the rascal down. That is radicalism working. But next I reflect that I may get myself in trouble, and then I do nothing to save the defenceless. That is conservatism. Conservatism thinks one thing and says another. A fat office will make a conservative still more conservative, that is make him afraid to squeak. I know men who are so scary about position, that they would swear that Andrew Johnson is the Tycoon of Japan if they thought that would keep them in office. A real guilty rebel hates a man who has so many tongues.

The spirit of the age is intensely radical. Majorities at the ballot-box show it. The increase of schools and churches proves it. Our people are not so bad, after all. The majority are good people, and 'adicals. The minority will soon succumb. When a majority is so good, and so strong, too, it must prevail. Surely all men will soon learn that all others have rights as well as themselves—and that is all the Radical party preaches. Radicalism will advance over the ruins of slavery and treason. The people will learn to do right between man and man, and peace and prosperity, secured by wise and wholesome laws, and not by the thunder of battle, will follow—and that right soon. And, concludes Mr. Gray:

"Men are growing tired of fighting against Right—the spirit of the age. Wrong and Oppression have marshaled their hosts, and their battle has been fought and lost. Right and Freedom are triumphant to-day. Men will learn how dearly tyrants pay for trying to oppress their fellow men. A sense of those higher Christian duties which each owes to the other will soon dawn on the yet darkened intellect of our race, and all men, moved by a good impulse, will yet 'do unto others as they would have others do unto them.'"

MR. GRAY'S NOTION OF A HOG IS VERY AMUSING.

The hog thinks a heap of himself, and hates you. A hog is a man that wants his own share of everything, and your share, too. He is generally a sole corporation without a soul. If he goes into business, he goes it by himself. If the hog takes anybody into partnership with him, he takes him in. He never studied grammar any further than "*mine*"—he left school before he got to "*thine*." He is full of parables. You never heard a better preacher than the hog. To hear the hog talk you would consider him a saint disguised in flesh, consenting to be a man for a while just to teach men how to live. But just wait till he acts once, and you will see he is a real swine, with the devil inside and a man's coat on the outside. The hog eats all he can reach. The hog does all the talking in the company. The hog never listens. The hog is always rooting the dirty mud up, and putting it on somebody's clean character with his ugly black snout, and goes along rooting and stinking, and grunting as he roots.

I want to be a hog,
And with the hoggies dwell.

OLD MEN VERSUS YOUNG MEN.

The prevailing idea is that old men are better than young men. It is false in fact, entirely false. Youth is full of fire and energy. Old age is stupid, cold, and slow of movement. Why could not old Halleck or old Scott do as well as young Grant or young Sheridan? The answer is simple—they were too old for use.

Is it not so in official positions here, too? Old fossils usurp the places of young blood and young brains. Of course, we would avoid extremes. Too young a man is zero. Too old a man is zero. But old age is venerable. True, it is and ought to be venerable, but old age should charge no money for being venerable. Old age is time for rest. Youth time for action. Decrepit age should make way for young blood and brains. When old fossils hang on too long, death, the friend and ally of human progress, sweeps old age into oblivion.

A THOUGHT.

Thought moves the world. Thought is God. Matter is the universe. Thought set it going, and keeps it going still. A thought of a man is a throb of his spirit. When spirits think they live. When spirits think not they are dormant, dead for the time. Thought springs from the brain, as the goddess sprung from the sea. Thought controls men. Thought makes watches and pins. Thought uses the steam and electricity which God made. It flows out of the brain, and makes the material world dance again. It leaps like lightning out of mind. A thought never dies. Immortality is stamped on every real thought, and it cannot die till God dies. To find out one of God's thoughts is to discover an island beautiful and grand in the boundless Godhead.

EXHAUSTION VERSUS SUGGESTION—PREACHERS.

I used to hear a very pious, but very simple old preacher preach every Sunday. The old man was very exhaustive. He was very learned and very diffuse. He never for a moment supposed his congregation knew anything except what he told them in his sermons. He would use up two hours of a hot summer Sunday proving that sin is wrong, that man is mortal, that God is good, or that hell is hot—just as if the merest child in the congregation was not already fully convinced, before he said a word. His sermons were exhaustive; they exhausted me, for many and many a long snooze I took under the awning of his preaching. And they exhausted the old man, too; for he took the sore throat, or something that way, and died, and now sleeps in the old church-yard, a victim to exhaustive preaching.

There are multitudes of preachers just like him—yes, and writers, too. They take up a subject and consider it objectively, and subjectively, and mentally, and morally, and physically, and proximately, and absolutely, and practically, and emblematically, and horizontally, and latitudinarily, and every other way, until they exhaust themselves and you. And so they think by bursting one of these learned bomshells over you to terify you with their mental power, but after all it's only smoke and dust, just like the bursting of a puff-ball.

We like suggestive writing and speaking. We love to be left to think for ourselves. We want no writer or speaker to do all our thinking for us. To touch and go, and sip the foam of many themes—this is our idea of agreeable and useful writing and speaking. Franklin is full of hints. Solomon is full of suggestions. You can take up Solomon's suggestions, or Franklin's hints, and think and think about them. Yes, the perfection of writing and speaking alike is to be full of suggestions.

HUE AND CRY.

The old common law process of pursuing with horn and with voice all felons, was adapted well to the day and age in which it was used. No sooner was a crime known to have been committed than pursuit was made from town to town, and from county to county, until the felon was taken and delivered to the sheriff. All the people were commanded to join in this hue and cry by voice and honr, and to follow the criminal on foot and on horses, blowing horns and crying aloud until the criminal was overtaken, apprehended, or killed. If the town or hundred failed to join in this public outcry and pursuit, action lay against the hundred.

Railroads, steamboats, and telegraphs have rendered this old-fashioned method useless, for now the hue and cry after the fleeing felon is made by the whistle of the steamer, the scream of the locomotive, and the lightning click of the telegraph. No man can outrun the steam or the lightning, and the public press simultaneously raises the hue and cry all over the land. Wherever the criminal flees, the hue and cry is around him, and he cannot escape it.

GOD.

Do you know what God is? I do not; I can comprehend a little of anything, but not much, for my capacity is very small. I could understand 2, 4, or 6, may be 99 or 100; but when it comes to a 1,000 or 1,000,000 at once, it is too much for my little mind. We are finite, but we can't comprehend all finite things. The national debt of billions I can say over, but I cannot comprehend it, and yet it is finite, that is, it is limited. My eyes can see a big picture, but not the whole sky, nor the whole sea, and yet these are finite. But there are God's thoughts more numerous than the dollars of our national debt; there is God's presence covering sea and sky, and more. If I had God's mind I could understand all his infinite and eternal attributes, but with my feeble powers, I can only view the infinitude of God, as a man born blind sees space.

SLEEP AND DREAMS.

Sitting alone in my room, I reasoned thus of sleep and dreams:

Philosophy, in vain, attempts to explain the mystery of sleep and dreams. They lie away beyond the boundaries of human reason. The waking mind seems to be one, and the sleeping mind another. The waking body seems to be one, and the sleeping body another. But it is the same mind, and it is the same body whether awake or asleep. But in sleep, the powers of the body are no longer obedient to the volitions of the mind. The form seems to be for a time divorced from its spiritual mate. The mind wanders off and forgets the body. The body breathes the air, circulates the blood, and passively awaits the return of the wandering spirit. When the spirit returns from its aerial flights, the body shakes off its slumbers, and arises. For a moment time and place seem strange. The awakened eye looks wonderingly for a little time at the real world before it, and it is only after an effort of the will, now master of soul and body again, that the clouds of the spiritual world are lifted from the vision, and one sees the tangible forms as they exist. With these half-formed views in my mind, I fell asleep. Sleep fell gently upon me, and my ears were closed to all terrestial sounds, and my eyes blind to all sublunary scenes, and my hand lay familiarly in the hand of the Invisible, while my spiritual eyes saw new intangible creations, and my ears drank in the very essence of music. I trod the soft floor of the infinite, while a blue sky, not round, spread itself, like an illimitable sea, before my view. I was no more " of the earth earthy," but purely spiritual. Corporeal things had vanished forever from me. The incorporeal essence of things, thought, and being, rolled its thin gauze around my soul. I was all soul. Body had perished, and lived not even in memory. The universe was no more a hard thing upon which to fall was to be crushed. It was soft, spiritual, light as air. One could drop through millions of miles of this canopy of spirituality and feel no more shock than he would from the act of breathing. There were no wings. The child's idea of cherubs and angels having wings seemed gross and absurd. All was thought. Thought needs no feathered wings, no more than light needs wings. To wish was to will, and to will to accomplish. One volition of the will transported one, quick as lightning, just as far as the soul would wish to go. This was sleep and dreams.

James M. Dalzell.

THE MOTHER'S PRAYER FOR HER SOLDIER BOYS.

An old man sits in his easy chair,
His eyes grown dim with years,
And the frosts of age are on his hair;
His cheeks are wet with tears.

The old man sits in his lonely chair,
His wife is long since dead;
His heart is full of an echoing prayer,
The last on earth she said!

" My two brave boys in thy mercy spare,
God, if it be thy will,
Wherever they may be to-night, there
Thy goodness guard them still."

Her spirit fled to the far sweet land-
Her boys had gone before ;
Up from the battle reaching a hand
To greet her on that shore.

The old man sits in his lonely chair,
His wife is long since dead ;
His heart is full as it echoes the prayer
The dying mother said.

J. M. DALZELL.

Contrast is what regulates our estimate of things. When this contrast is strongly marked, we call it novel. A long succession of occurrences of the same kind wearies us. But let the scenes be shifted, and we are somehow delighted at the change, let it be what it may. This is the leaven that keeps the world working—the desire of change is what makes change, as the desire for heirs causes their procreation.

But what we most desire to look at now is this reality of life. Whatever costs us labor, soon becomes irksome, for we naturally love ease. The real duties of life will often be found to conflict with our own wishes. "Necessity knows no law," and by the sweat of our brows must we earn our bread. This is the rule that governs mankind—whether they will love it or not, they must obey it.

Physical man needs exercise to keep the vital machinery in healthful play, and this exercise in some way or another must be employed in gaining subsistence for the body—the feeding of the stomach is at last the grand ultimatum of human labor. Some preconceit of the thing destroys our capacity for investigating and understanding its essence. We will carry a kaleidescope and see things all discolored and distorted, when, if we would look at them with the clear eyes God has given us, we could see them just as they are. Every one designs and projects plans and purposes foreign to his taste or his abilities. It was well for Alexander to be Alexander, because he could be nothing else ; but we, in attempting to be Alexanders shall probably be nothings. And it is not improper to plan and purpose early and well, and to these to adhere with diligent perseverance, but this mapping out of a future course in life should be the legitimate offspring of a careful and thorough self-examination, and a correct knowledge of our own powers and possibilities. If the unreasoning hap-hazard self will have me do the thing, I shall ask judgment to show me why, and how, first of all, the end shall be attained. No more common error besets our paths than this, that my strongest desire is the index of my ability to do. But we shall not forget that the critics show us that the mistakes arising from this is what makes the lowest comedy. A man of eighty, by some hallucination, is led to imagine that he is strong, agile, and handsome. Under this delusion goes into society to play the gallant, and the poor, deluded old fool becomes the by-word and the sport of the rosy young damsels, who tolerate his ridiculous attentions for the amusement that he affords them. My desires and my abilities may be as widely separated as those of the old man just cited. No, this is not the rule. Put him at what he likes best, is a fossilized adage that nine times in ten puts the man out of the way of doing the only one thing he can do well. Universal genius is like the diamond—it is scarce and precious, and easily detected. But the most of us have but limited minds. We must not attempt too much, or we shall do nothing. For this reason the old temple had written above its doors, " Know thyself." To know this is to know our whole power and duty. My bowels will listen to no sophistry, and as Emerson says, " the belly will not be reasoned down." O, Stoics, how have ye failed, inasmuch as all your false formulas could never make a starving wretch think he had been well fed. Epicureans, tugging at the other extreme of Error's lengthened chain, how have the gross vessels of the animal man discomfited you, and vomited back in your very teeth the superfluous trash with which your philosophy had burdened them. " The last feather breaks the camel's back," says the proverb, and the moral of this, as applied to the wants of men, would seem to be, that more than enough is as bad as less than enough, and that breaks down the system by its superfluous weight, as the other suffers it to decay by reason of its insufficiency. What we want is a golden mean in all the economics.

Most of us see nature through a glass darkly; I mean most of us do not allow our mental eyes to look at the naked principles of nature.

What should we think of the mariner who would leave a good, sound ship, his accustomed track upon the sea, and embark on unknown waters in a crazy old vessel, and without a compass, and all this merely to gratify a whim? And yet, thousands do precisely this on the sea of life, without consulting age and experience as well as their own minds, hearts, nerves, blood, and limbs—

without standing face to face honestly with self, and trying to see if the means and the end are in any rational relation to each other, we rush into things either to gratify our own wrong prejudices and bad passions, or otherwise to gratify cunning or foolish counsellors. If a man should advise me to fly, I would laugh at his gratuitous folly, but should be very sorry to make the attempt of flying from the church steeple. And so if he should advise me to undertake some mission for which I had no manner of fitness, or to enter some office or profession which was either dishonorable, worthless or hazardous, would I not be quite as foolish to take that advice as the other?

If we take cool and judicious glances at the things that surround us, and measure with a careful eye the forces that are in us, we shall generally find scope for all we can do of any given work. First comes the survey of the land, marking out the metes and boundaries of the field in which our short life is to be spent; then comes the preparation for the work, then the work, and last of all the results. The agriculturalist, standing face to face with nature's stern truths all the time, more nearly follows her bidding than any other man. He prepares the ground in due season and with great care, sows good seed in good ground, and cultivates the ground while the tender corn is growing, and leaves the rest to God until the harvest time. If in other things there were such method in our labor, what grand results could be attained. Some begin at the wrong end. Expect a harvest before any labor is done.

ROMANCE AND REALITY.

Reality may be fitly compared to the broad, blue sky; and romance to the occasional clouds that flit across it. Reality is oftener found than romance. Indeed this is the chief excellence of romance, that it is rarely seen. I have not much notion that life would afford us much pleasure in the aggregate, if all sorrow and pain were banished from the world. We would then never, it is true, be tormented with any mental or physical suffering; but life would be one unvaried succession of insipid pleasures. Constituted as our frames now are, a more desirable state of things than that we now live in cannot be conceived. We are planed, mortised, and built in with the rest of God's works. We may mourn over the wants and weakness of humanity, struggle on vigorously among the waves that we know shall at last swallow us; and with eyes almost blinded and hands almost palsied, hope against hope, and fight against fate—this is the reality of life.

Romance rears palaces in the clouds, opens cooling fountains in the Sahara, and makes things seem other than they are. Romance throws enchantment around everything that the heart may desire, and almost uniformly deceives its infatuated followers. Attachments the most sacred in name, but the most vile in essence, are often formed through the magic influence of romance. Would it not be romantic? Then, by the gods, I will attempt it. This is the philosophy of unphilosophic youth. It is the tempter and destroyer of virtue, truth, and happiness. Youth does not ask what is " the true, the beautiful, and the good," but what is the strange and wonderful. The stern truths of history, the mild teachings of philosophy, the abstract reasonings of pure mathematics—how quickly are these left for the " Lamp of Aladdin," " Jack the Giant Killer," or " Goody Two Shoes." This is the period of memory and imagination, of staring wonder and marvellous fancy. It runs on into manhood, too, sometimes, and when indulged merely as a pastime, and not entertained with earnestness and avidity, and pursued with unreasoning diligence, romance has its uses. It is a beautiful pastime. It is a painter that frescoes as well the cottage of the peasant as the palace of the king. It fills the sky, the sea, the earth, and even the illimitable region of mind with pictures sublimer and grander far than any of Apelles or Raphael.

For, if eighteen hours out of the twenty-four the black clouds frown upon us, and the other six are illumed with sunshine or gemmed with stars, or crowned with rainbows, we shall love these six hours the more, and enjoy them the better.

At times all is quiet in nature, scarce a leaf moves in all the forest, and the greatest sound we hear is the chirp of the cricket, or, perhaps, the cheerful warbling of the thrush. But on comes the storm apace; the zephyr at first gently rustling the myriad leaves of the forest, growing into a gale, swelling into a storm, and mounting at last into a terrific hurricane, screaming and howling to the wild accompaniment of the sublime thunders that burst peal upon peal from the great batteries of heaven. The scene thus presented suddenly to us awakes the most sublime and the noblest feelings. We are filled with wonder, and stand in mute and sacred astonishment in the presence of the unveiled forces of nature. *   *   *   * Young men, scarcely out of college, grasp at positions designed alone for age and experience. Of course they fail. Others see fitness in themselves for things that they cannot do; others see in themselves a capacity that no other man can see. In short, a great multitude elect themselves to places where God never designed they should be, and where they never will be.

Romance lies at the bottom of all these fatal delusions. What Fancy produces that the hand attempts to grasp, but too often finds, when it is too late for amendment, that the glittering toy is filled with ashes. I could wish myself such a man as he, the hero of the story that I have just read. I get the fancy into my brain somehow, that I can equal or surpass him. Following my ideal of perfect manhood with diligent imitation for years, I at length find that I am upon the wrong track; I have some things which he had and some which he had not, but I finally discover that that one thing which I lack, was just the very means by which he succeeded—so I stop short discouraged. In vain I try to work after some other model. My young, fresh ardor is lost, and I do not, if I can, attain to any measure of success at anything. So my will is puzzled, my hands and my brain paralyzed, my ambition and self-confidence gone, and I settle down, thinking I have tried hard my best powers, and if they can do no good, why then it is of no use to fall back upon my second rate talents. Useful lives are thus lost, as battles are lost by rash and ill-planned attacks. Can another point out the exact mathematical measure of my abilities? Or must I judge all about it myself? Others, to be sure, and especially my enemies will mark my blunders as they fall, and hold them up to the derisions of the mob. I can learn much by hearing what my enemies say of my blunders, and what my circle of friends tell about my merits. Putting these together, letting judicious and calm thought try all their opinions by the best rules within my reach, I can learn much that I ought to know. What others advise me to do, if judgment approves, that I should attempt. But if a man fails in a thing for a long time, is he to persevere in it, or turn to something else? There is another momentous question. Failures will often attend the wisest and noblest efforts. "There is no such word as fail in the vocabulary of man." "What man has done man can do." These two aphorisms, however clothed in words, always come up to the mind of the determined but unfortunate adventurer. But there is much falsehood, ruinous counsel in both, inasmuch as the one encourages a blind perseverance, even to inevitable ruin, while the other is nothing but a lie. Man cannot do whatever man has done. Thousands of men stand out as heroes in history, whose lives and actions have been parodied by herds of unsuccessful imitators in all ages. No, no, if you can perform some great feat, which it is out of my power to do, I can never do it, and that is all of it. But how shall I know before I try? Very well—one should know his own capacity, and then judge, if it be in his power, to accomplish the required task; and if it be worthy of him, and not an idle whim, he should attempt it, and he will accomplish it. The old by-the-way of the Latins, the qualifying word for almost any proposed possibility, is a good thing to remember "*cæteris paribus.*" This done, let the critics hiss while I whistle!

We are indebted to Hon. D. S. Gibbs, Probate Judge of Noble county, Ohio, for a copy of the will of John Gray. The will, as every one knows, could not be probated until after the death of the testator. The will was probated April 16, 1868, and reads as follows:

COPY OF JOHN GRAY'S WILL.

In the name of the Benevolent Father of all, I, John Gray, of the county of Noble, and State of Ohio, being now in the 104th year of my age, of sound mind and memory, though my limbs are feeble, and I am the last survivor of the Revolutionary war.

Item 1. I give and devise to my only daughter, Nancy McElroy, and heirs, forever, all the moneys, goods, chattels, and effects, of whatsoever kind or nature, that may be in my possession at the time of my decease, only asking that she, the beloved Nancy, will still continue to take care of me while I live, as she has done heretofore. And the above devise is made to compensate so far as I am able the said Nancy McElroy for the care, kindness, and attention that I always have received at her hands.

Item 2. I do hereby revoke all former wills by me made. In testimony whereof I hereunto set my hand and seal this 14th day of February, 1867. JOHN GRAY. [SEAL.]

Signed and acknowledged by said John Gray, as his last will and testament, in our presence, and signed by us in his presence.
PHILIP BURLINGAME,
JOHN W. SCOTT.

A true copy from the records of the court.

D. S. GIBBS,
[SEAL.] *Probate Judge, Noble county, Ohio.*

The following beautiful poem is from the pen of an esteemed brother Sigma Chi—J. Wickliffe Jackson, the poet. When I was returning from my visit to John Gray last summer, I met brother Jackson at Wheeling, and we came through together to Washington. I had met this kind brother before on the occasion of the last Biennial Convention of the Sigma Chi at Dr. Samson's. It will be remembered that on that occasion he was the poet of the day. When I met brother Jackson at Wheeling, he was returning from the commencement of Indiana State University, where he had delivered a poem at the request of our brothers Sigma Chi. He is, perhaps, the most distinguished poet in our fraternity, and one of whom we are justly proud. Brothers Samson, Wahl, Devol, Dixon, Murray, Meredith, Weills, and all the rest of my brothers will bear me out in this assertion:

On our way to Washington, I related John Gray's story to brother Jackson, and he promptly transformed it by the talismanic touch of genius into the following "rhythmical creation of beauty," which I here insert alike in honor of John Gray and the Sigma Chi:

[From the Noble County, Ohio, Republican.]

JOHN GRAY.

BY J. WICKLIFFE JACKSON, OF WILMINGTON, DEL.

[John Gray, the subject of this Poem is, according to the records of the War Department, the last man of the Revolution. He now resides in Brookfield township, this county, and will be 104 years of age next January.—Ed. Republican.]

I.

One by one the severed links have started
  Bonds that bound us to the sacred past;
One by one, our patriot sires departed,
  Time hath brought us to behold the last:
Last of all who won our early glory,
  Lonely traveller of the weary way,
Poor, unknown, unnamed in song or story,
  In his western cabin, lives John Gray.

Deign to stoop to rural shades, sweet Clio!
  Sing the hero of the sword and plow:
On the borders of his own Ohio,
  Weave a laurel for the veteran's brow,
While attuned until the murmuring waters
  Flows the burden of thy pastoral lay.
Bid the fairest of Columbia's daughters,
  O'er his locks of silver, crown John Gray.

Slaves of self and serfs of vain ambition,—
  Toilful strivers of the city's mart,
Turn awhile, and bless the sweet transition,
  Unto scenes that soothe the careworn heart;
Turn with me, to yonder moss thatched dwelling,
  Wreathed in woodbine and the wild-rose spray;
While the muse his simple tale is telling,
  Tottering on his crutches, see John Gray.

II.

When defeat had pressed his bitter chalice
  To the lips of England's haughty lord,—
Bowed in shame the brow of stern Cornwallis,
  And at Yorktown claimed his bloody sword:
At the crowning of the seige laborious—
  At the triumph of the glorious day,
Near his chieftain, in the ranks victorious,
  Stood the youthful soldier, brave John Gray.

While he vowed through peace their love should burn on—
  While he bade his tearful troops farewell;
One alone unto thy shades, Mount Vernon,
  Called the Chieftain with himself, to dwell.
Proud to serve the Father of the Nation,
  Glad to hear the voice that bade him stay,
Year by year upon the broad plantation,
  Unto ripened manhood, toiled John Gray.

Sowed and reaped and gathered to the garner
  All the Summer plenty's golden sheaves,—
Sowed and reaped, till Time the ruthless warner
  Whispered through the dreary autumn leaves:
" Wherefore tarry ? Freedom's skies are o'er thee:
  Winter frowneth ere the blush of May:
Lo! Is not a goodly land before thee?
  Up! and choose thee now a home, John Gray."

III.

Thus he heard the words of duty's warning,
  And he saw the rising Empire-star
Dawning dimly on the nation's morning—
  Guiding westward Emigration's car:
Heard and saw and quickly rose to follow,
  Bore his rifle for the savage prey,
Bore his axe, that soon in greenwood hollow
  Timed thy sylvan ballads, bold John Gray.

Blessed with love, his lonely labors cheering,
  Blithe the hearthstones of that forest nook,
Where arose his cabin in the " clearing,"
  Near the meadow with its purling brook :
Where his children from their noonday laughter
  Turned at eve and left their joyous play,
Hushed and still, when the great hereafter
  Spake the Christian father, meek John Gray.

IV.

Oh, the years of mingled joy and sadne
  Oh, the hours—the countless hours of toil,
Shared alike through sorrow and through gladness
  By loved hands now mouldering in the soil;
Oh, the anguish stifled in the shadow
  Of the gloom that bore *her form* away!
'Neath yon mound she slumbers in the meadow,
  Waiting, meekly waiting thee, John Gray.

All day long upon the threshold sitting,
  Where the sunbeams through the bright leaves shine—
Where the zephyrs, through his white locks flitting,
  Softly whispers of "the days lang syne,"
How he loves on holy thoughts to ponder;
  How his eyes the azure heaven survey,
Or toward yon meadow dimly wander:—
  Yes, beside her thou shalt sleep, John Gray!

In the tomb thy comrades' bodies slumber,—
  Unto heaven their souls have flown before;
Only one is "missing" of their number,—
  Only one to win the radiant shore:—
Only one to join the sacred chorus,—
  Only one to burst the bounds of clay:
Soon the sentry's trumpet sounding o'er us,
  To their ranks shall summon thee, John Gray.

V.

Peace be with thee—gentle spirits guard thee,
  Noble type of heroes now no more!
In thine age may gratitude reward thee,
  In thy need may bounty bless thy store;
Care of woman, gentle, true, and tender,
  Strength of manhood be thy guide and stay;
Let not those who roll in idle splendor,
  To their shame, forget thee, lone John Gray.

Five-score winters on thy head have whitened—
  Five-score summers o'er thy brow have passed:
All the sunshine that thy pathway brightened,
  Clouds of want and care have overcast,
Thus the last of those who won our glory,
  Lonely traveller of the weary way,
Poor, unknown, unnamed in song or story.
  In his western cabin, lives John Gray.

WILMINGTON, DEL., *Sept.* 11, 1867.

WASHINGTON AND GRANT.

A Birth-day Ode, delivered before the Irving Lyceum, at City Hall, Washington, D. C., February 22, 1868, by James M. Dalzell, a member of the Lyceum :

INVOCATION.

Ye spirits that around the Rocky mountains roam,
And on the Blue Ridge summits rear your cloudy dome,
Or in the deepest shades of western forests keep,
Or rock the storms upon " the cradle of the deep:"
Ye genii dwelling in the cis-Atlantic caves,
Or waving golden banners o'er Pacific's waves,
Or singing down the Mississippi's silver line,
Or musing sweetly where the great lakes' waters shine;
Ye children of the far prairie's floral plain,
Where Beauty, Mirth, and Harmony forever reign—
Ye guardian angels of my dear, my native land,
Some noble inspiration give—O, guide this trembling hand.
On this the natal day of him whose valor won
Our Freedom—this the natal day of Washington.

PROEM.

Washington ! a name familiar to us all
As that our mother called us by : a name
As oft repeated 'round the family hearth
As that of mother, home, and heaven.
Washington ! familiar is the grand old name,
The sweetest name the world hath learned, and still
Wherever floats fair freedom's flag there swells
From patriot tongues the name of Washington.
The child just risen from it's mother's knee,
And standing first upon the sacred soil,
First learns to lisp with reverent awe
The awful Name above all names—and then
The next name learned is that of Washington.
The old man, folding up his meek pale hands,
And making ready for the sleep of Death,
In accents trembling with his dying breath,
His weeping children bids to serve the Lord,
And still be true to that bright banner
Which first became the cherished symbol of
A people's freedom in the hands of Washington.
In every cabin in the western wilds,
In every palace in the eastern world—
By every tongue, in every land beneath the sun,
Where human hearts are fond of liberty,
Evermore resounds the name of Washington.
Familiar as the name is grown to men,
They love to hear it sounding yet, and still
As ages pass, and kingdoms fall, and right prevails,
And nations grow more free, and proud, and glad,
The airs of freedom to the echoes joined
Will cover all the earth with one sweet sound
In harmonies combined, repeating Washington.
'Tis fitting, then, that we, on this his natal day,
Should celebrate the birth of Washington,
Recalling what he did and dared for us

And all the heirs of that bright heritage
Carved from despot hands by his bright sword
'Tis fitting that we here recall his virtues,
And record, though with imperfect muse,
Our love for our own Washington.

       O, come,
Ye lofty spirits from the fields of song,
In all your "singing robes" and flowing train:
And voices chanting out melodeous verse,
And us inspire with fitting thought, and words
Aglow with some of that seraphic fire
Which made such glowing harmony on the lips
Of Otis, Henry, Adams, Jefferson,
When they with fervent praise of Washington,
With kindling eloquence, in Freedom's name
Proclaimed him leader of their glorious cause.
And there is one, another Washington,
Whose fame with his the hands of fate have joined.
And while the name of Washington is named
By patriot tongues, another mighty name
Shall ring with grandeur thro' our fair domain:
And Freedom's sons can ne'er forget the chief
Who saved the flag from rebel hands, and now
Is still defending with a hero's might
The flag of Washington, of you and me,
Need I repeat in blind and staggering verse,
And accents rude, and numbers illy tuned
That chieftain's name which echoes now
In verse and prose throughout the land !
Need my imperfect muse repeat the name
Of him who flung our banner to the breeze of War
And by it stood through all the fiery storm,
Thundering with the might of Jove at Treason's gate,
Far down the Mississippi's bloody stream;
Or turning to the East when Vicksburg fell,
To drive the traitor from his last foul den,
And wrest the bloody sword from Traitor hands
At Appamattox, and so close the war !
Ah, no ; that name is written in the nation's heart
That name is sacred to the army yet,
And Freedom stands with Victory now,
And, smiling, both are crowning him with fame,
And all the loyal land repeat Grant's name.

FIRST IN WAR.

Foremost among the mighty names that make
The times of Revolution brilliant yet,
Chief of all that patriot host that won
For us our freedom, and our glorious flag,
"First in War," the brightest spirit of them all—
Behold the Chieftain, Washington ;
A man not moulded in a lordly hall,
Nor reared in splendor near a kingly throne,
Nor taught to jabber in a classic shade,
Nor trained for War by printed rules :
But in the wilderness of this far land,
Born and nurtured in the plainest scenes
That plain and rugged Nature can provide,
To manly independence every thought attuned,
And every act conformed to Nature's plan.
And all the man controlled by love of Right,
His great heart full of love to God, and man,
He grew up strong in body, strong in mind,
In purpose strong, and armed with right.

God and the people holding up his hands.
And guiding and supporting him through all.
He took the Army, and Victory loved
To leave the tyrant and to come to him.

FIRST IN PEACE.

And when the war-clouds rolled away,
And all the Nation's sky was bright with Peace,
He, the "First in War," the conquering chief,
The brave, resistless General became
Again the First, the "First in Peace,"
And at the Nation's helm, in Peace again,
Saul-like, with head and shoulders over all,
The grandest, greatest President he stood,
And words of wisdom from the cherished chief
Still guided our young nation's early plans,
And every danger he foresaw and turned
The Ship of State around ere she had touched
The rocks of discord lying near.
His Farewell to the people whom he loved,
His Farewell words still linger yet, and oft
With tender memories rushing though the mind
Do millions read those Farewell words—
Words of counsel caught from heaven,
Words of hope and words of cheer,
The last words of the great immortal chief,
While Americans still love the land he loved,
And still revere the flag to him so dear.
Will his words linger in the people's hearts,
And guide the people's hands, and keep
Still sacred and secure, the liberties
Wrung for us from tyrants' hands,
And first made safe by Washington.

FIRST IN THE HEARTS OF HIS COUNTRYMEN.

Millions have lived and died since the tomb
Closed first upon the corpse of Washington.
That corpse in marble wastes, and dries to common dust,
And ashes now are all we have of Washington.
Though he is dead and gone to the dust,
His spirit lives, and breathes in all our laws,
And is the talismanic word that makes these States
In harmony and Union ever ONE.
The Declaration, Constitution, Laws,
The Union, Flag, and Nation's Arms,
Are bound in volumes with a golden thread
That reaches through the people's hearts,
Is fastened to the throne of God, and runs
All through the frame of Washington.
Let marble blush if it would tell
How dear is Washington to every heart:
His memory is not encased in stolid stone,
Nor pent up in your marble monument—
It lives in living men, and every tide
Of warm life-blood in every heart
Still murmurs sweetly as it courses on,
And all its crimson streams are vocal
With the praise of Washington.

www.ingramcontent.com/pod-product-compliance
Lightning Source LLC
Chambersburg PA
CBHW031246260626
47169CB00007B/2475